Two Sides
Carry on Circle

First Edition

Amazon KDP
ISBN: 9798320310268
Imprint: independently published

★: appears when you should switch to the opposite
story. Think of these books like a movie and its
changing scenes. You DON'T NEED to read both
sides of the story to understand what's going on
either.

Table of contents

"Don't think we won't kick this door in!" shouted
Scott

crack

"God Brynn be quiet." Zed whispered

"I'm sorry that there is a branch right here."
she rolled her eyes

Headlights shined into the bushes where the
Carry on Circle laid. Halle's eyes appeared over the
shrubs to see more bodies running to surround the
room.

"Guns grab the guns and circle around the
back." Scott ordered as the rest of the crew pulled
up

"Come on, we need to get out of here! We
can sneak out from where they just came from." Zay
said

"Just one more minute." Halle mumbled

"Kick it in!" Beth yelled

Halle motioned "Go go now"

Carry on Circle hid in the shadows and
dodged through the leaves. They could hear faint
yelling from the back. Not knowing where to go
now their best option was to hide in plain sight.
They escaped this time but the next isn't
guaranteed.

1
Where it all started

The sounds of music and bass bounced off the walls. A single joint changed multiple hands of people sitting on the ground.

"5,998, 5999, 6000! 6 G's baby…" Brynn exclaimed as she finished the final stack of cash

Zay swooped in and grabbed the multiple stacks of banded cash and handed them off to Zed

"Took you long enough." Zed laughed as he went to put the cash in the safe in the bedroom.

"Next time don't put the dumb one in charge of counting a big amount." Kaydon mumbled from one of the corners of the room

The door creaked open slowly. Zay and Zed swiveled their heads towards the door and were prepared to jump.

Zay sighed "Oh it's just Halle."

She waved the key in his face and rolled her eyes "You knew I was coming back from Marcos and Gabriel's."

"Was Antonio over there?" Zed asked

Halle chuckled "Pff no the last place he would be is his dad and cousins."

She walked over to Kaydon's corner and looked over his shoulder

He shifted the computer for her to see

She smirked "So now I'm Sarah, Brynn is Jen, Zay is Tommy, and so on and so forth."

"What do we need more ID's for?!" Zay asked, "We already have drawers full."

"We have to get our money somehow." He turned back to Halle "I'm thinking of expanding and opening this ID making business up. It does us no good to just use this for us and everyone Antonio is involved with. If we start selling ID's we could make an extra chunk of change."

Halle exchanged looks with the rest of the group. "I mean that would be something you would have to bring up with Antonio if you are planning on bringing more people in."

"Why? he's never here anyways!" Kaydon argued

Zay mumbled from across the room "It's not easy being the one at fault for all of us."

Kaydon scoffed "You're kidding right? He would be the first one to throw all of us under the bus."

"Antonio wouldn't do that. He is loyal to us and we are loyal to him. He wouldn't be anywhere without us." Halle shared

Kaydon shut his laptop "Yeah loyalty...because he has people who can't live without him. I'll be back later." He shut the door with power

A knock echoed off the door and Marcos' head peered in "Everything okay in here? Kaydon just passed me angrily down the stairs."

"Yeah everything g." Zed replied as he walked back in the living room.

Marcos motioned to Halle "I bring news. Antonio and Tricky are going to be stopping by later so make sure nobody else is around at like 4am."

"Where are we supposed to sleep then?" Brynn asked

Zay replied "Yeah that's ridiculous the Carry on Circle lives here so we should be able to stay and see our *ringleaders*."

"I thought you didn't have direct contact with them?" Zed added on

Marcos stuttered, "He called from a payphone."

Zay fired back "Who's he?"

the phone rang

Zed looked down at Marcos pocket "You finna get that?"

"Can you guys lay off the third degree?" Halle chimed in

Marcos opened the door "You guys, the main group is welcome to stay with my dad and I tonight. Just you guys, not the rest of the randoms. I'll see you guys later."

Halle watched the door shut "We are not doing that."

"Where are we going to go then?" Brynn asked

"I don't trust Gabriel." Halle stated

"Chill Halle he's not just Anotnio's dad he's practically all of our dad." Zay replied

"Whatever but I'm not going. Even when I was just over there he stayed in the bathroom the whole time probably just poppin pills. Besides, why are we busting our balls for someone who we don't even see anymore!"

"Because he **is** family Halle. He gives us a place to live and a career path." Zay said

She scoffed "Some career path."

The night time soon fell and the Carry on Circle gathered in the laundry room. Zed rolled a joint on one of the ironing boards. Halle and Brynn sat on top of one of the machines as he handed it off to them.

Brynn coughed up smoke as she passed it over to Halle.

Without a single thought Halle passed it over to Zay

"You don't want a hit?" Zay questioned

"You guys know I don't do that anymore. It's not cool that you guys keep trying to test a relapse."

Zed chuckled as he took his turn "It's just weed it ain't going to do anything."

Halle pushed past them into the darkness

The condo complex was a lot eerier in the night rather than the day. The streets crawled with roamers that would do anything to stay hidden from the light. The Carry on Circle thrived at night. They weren't like the other members where they had to hustle at night to stay alive. Halle, Zay, Zed, and Brynn have this time to recover from the anxiety filled sunlight. Most of the time things were pretty chill...until Antonio came around.

2
"Antonio"

Earlier that day

"Dude I'm not kidding you have to listen to me." Tricky stated as he fanned the smoke out of his face

Antonio yawned "You're trippin to hard and you're now ruining my trip. We are safe here plus we aren't wanted right now."

"Pff right now...We are always wanted! I missed court and you are still on the streets."

Antonio took another rip "Relax. We got miles of desert around us, guns, and some hardcore people who would do anything not to go back to jail."

Tricky bent down to get within eye level of his best friend. He whispered what only the two of them could hear "Those people out there would give you up in a heartbeat. Those people who are going to protect us will just get us into more trouble. We have to start running again and leave everything behind. It's the only way to look out for ourselves.

Tonio bro you got a baby at home and a chic who loves you. Just turn yourself in and be better for your family."

"First you were telling me that we need to take off again to avoid jail but now you switched up saying I need to go back to jail. Fuck you man."

Tricky rolled his eyes "You don't even know what you're saying. It's always just been you and me but now it's just me. I'm going back to my moms for a while and I'll let you figure your shit out. I ain't going to law enforcement either. That is if they don't take me first."

Antonio watched Tricky walk out of the room with just a single backpack. One last hit before the smoke knocked him out...

...Am I the Victim? Am I the criminal? I guess I can say I've played both parts. It's the typical villain origin story. Mom dead at 5 ½, Drugged dad, kids running the streets. I went anywhere really just to be wanted. My sister is the only good one out of us Mendonzas. She has her demons but not compared to my brother and I. Our sister played mommy at a young age literally and metaphorically. This story doesn't start though till I was about 16.

I was glued to my skateboard because it was my escape from home. I mostly rode in allies jumping trash cans or in rural areas.

I've lived in Los Campos my whole life, always loyal to the East side. If you were to ask me out of the four which one is my favorite. The East side is the only correct answer. The North and

South sides are filled with rich pricks who think they run the world. The West side...gotta love it but I ain't tryna get shot simply for stepping a toe over the county line. With any big city there are mainly two sections, the rich and the poor. One day I might see the rich but I'll never come up the same way they do. Every big city has their secret societies that hide in the shadows. That's where you go to feel wanted. The big struggle is finding them.

The afternoon sun beat down on the asphalt. I had just landed a trick I had been working on in my favorite hidden ally until I heard a familiar sound. I hid behind a larger dumpster to listen to the skateboard tracks pass me. I peaked around the corner to see the backs of two guys rounding the corner.

I quickly dropped my board and rode as fast as I could to catch up with them. Weaving in and out of traffic I stayed a little ways behind them in hopes they wouldn't notice me.

A few minutes later we ended up at the old courthouse on the border of the East Side. There were hundreds of skaters from all over the city. All the cement and walls were covered in graffiti. The two skaters disappeared before my eyes but it seems like I ended up in the right place.

All of a sudden two arms grabbed me and I was dragged behind one of the graffiti walls. Just as I was about to start swinging the guy and I made eye contact.

"Marcos? What the hell are you doing?!"

"Oh sorry primo. We just saw somebody followin us and we had to react. This is my buddy Jacob. Jacob, this is my cousin Antonio."

Jacob extended his knuckles for a fist bump "Hey man! Have you been here before?"

Antonio shook his head

"Well this is technically illegal so don't go spreading the word." Marcos replied

"What makes it illegal?" Antonio asked

Jacob answered "Since this is an abandoned place they like to charge anyone over here with trespassing; even if you don't go inside."

"Yeah they like to ruin everyone's fun. If you talk to the right people they'll hook you up with trustworthy goods." Marcos said

"What goods? You're two years younger than me?!"

Jacob pointed to a cluster of boulders under a tree "And you see that. Heaven on earth right there. Chics who are super chill and like to smoke plus they always know where the next bangin parties are at."

I chuckled and dropped my board on the floor "Let's go then!"

The sun couldn't be warmer as it began to set. Cruising down the concrete everyone waved to each other and welcomed me in. This was the beginning of hopefully my new forever. Finally a place where I felt loved and wanted just by a first meeting.

Soon enough I started spending all my afternoons there. I loved getting closer with my cousin who was more of a brother to me than my actual one. I also gained another brother too. Jacob, Marcos, and I slowly became inseparable. I trusted these guys with my life and they felt the same towards me.

Every so often the cops would show up and the adrenaline rush was unbeatable running from them. A wall of trust was beginning to be built between me and a lot of other people. After a while it started to become less fun when I was the only sober one.

So what did I do...?

I joined my first smoke circle

A first smoke circle turned into a first pill

Drugs then mixed with alcohol

Soon enough it was whatever I could get my hands on. But it was fine because I trusted these people so these things were not putting me in harm. It was just all good fun.

Besides Marcos started way before me

It wasn't long before I started getting into trouble when my older sister, Salia, was always there to bail me out.

My dad was still doing his thing running the streets so no matter where I went I was exposed to this. Even though Marcos and Jacob welcomed me in, it still felt like it was them two then me. It wasn't long before Tricky started skating at the courthouse.

Tricky was known for his ties to 19th West and running his block in the West side. Believe it or not that gave him an abundant amount of street cred. Everyone wanted to be his friend because they knew they could get something from him.

I don't know how but I grew closer with Tricky. We bonded over losing a parent and being able to suck it up to continue living. It wasn't long before we became the iconic duo of Antonio and Tricky.

Marcos' parents were absent a lot so he began living with us. We had drifted apart so it was nice to still have that cousin bond going home.

Eventually the four of us came together and we were the top dogs. I had girls all over me but one stood out to me. This was Maria. I regret how our relationship went and I guess I could blame the drug but that wouldn't be 100% truthful. Wow...Maria...every time I think back to this time in my life she was the most smokin hot girl with the most smokin hot personality. I was smitten with her but of course I couldn't let anyone see that. She had her group of friends too but it was clear she was the star; at least in my eyes.

Not only was it the iconic duo of Antoio and Tricky but the iconic couple of Antonio and Maria.

I would kill for that girl and my world was complete once I found out she felt the same. She was someone who I couldn't live without and i didnt want to spend my life with anyone else.

For the first time my life seemed perfect. I had a close group of friends, a girlfriend I loved with my whole heart, street cred, and so much more.

Unfortunately though what is up must come down.

My dad was very open to Jacob, Tricky, and Maria living with us but they all had homes too so they only stayed with us occasionally. I didn't know much about Jacobs' home life because he never talked about it much. It was an unspoken rule to never ask anyone about their home life so I never asked. Tricky practically became a Mendoza though. Maria had a lot of self control when it came to drugs and alcohol but us boys had a free for all every time. Especially Jacob. What I can remember is every time he would come over or when we would skate he would reach his limit as fast as he could and not leave until he was mostly sobered up.

Each time his limit increased a little bit more with testing fate just a little bit more too.

I didn't know that day would be the last day I saw him breathing. I didn't know that pill would kill him. Everyone around me told me it was an accident but deep down...I knew I killed Jacob.

We each tried this new pill that my dad had gotten from somebody but little did we know Jacob was already high on something else.

By the time it hit him it was too late.

I can't remember much from that day mainly from the trauma blocking but also the pill had some sort of memory loss.

None of us ever talk about it or even bring up Jacob's name. It wasn't until the day of the funeral I found out who Jacob actually was.

I attended the funeral but came late and left early. I had my own reasoning and I didnt even get a chance to say goodbye. That was on purpose though. Marcos was the only person who truly knew Jacob and where he came from. I had no idea he came from the family of the famous bounty hunters in Los Campos. Thinking back it all makes so much sense though.

I remember being in the very back and seeing his entire family in the front row. All their faces I have seen before. Never did I think one day they would be hunting me. They tried to get me before and they had an idea I had ties to Jacob but I got myself out of it. Still don't know how but it was taken care of. My older brother though wasn't so lucky. To this day I don't know if he's out of jail but he's far away from home.

There was a time during the funeral that I made eye contact with his dad and I had that burning sensation in my heart that he knew it was me. I guess the world really is full circle.

For some reason though after that day I became the leader of everything. Nobody knew I was the one who gave Jacob the pill and I wanted to keep it like that. Nobody knew that was the reason it took his life. However they knew though that my family had good shit. In a way I outshined Tricky but I knew he didn't mind that.

Jacob never was involved with The Carry on Circle but I knew he would have loved it.

I know this may be fucked up to say but I dont regret what I did. How was I supposed to know that was going to be the outcome? Everything happens for a reason and he died having a good time. I have to say though when I get high and start thinking about the old days it comes back to haunt me. It can be pretty hard to get out of that mindset too but there's always a drug to fix that.

✳✳✳✳

"Yo man are yuh guud? We can't call 911 out here so you better wake yo ass up."

Antonio's vision came back, blurry, but enough to see the outline of the leader of the ranch standing over him. He grunted some forms of life.

"Ight jus checkin to make shore yur still alive brother."

"I can't get high like that anymore. The memories are starting to haunt me." Antonio replied in a mix of words

"You gots to smoke through the pain. We all have demons inside us but we suffocate them with smoke!"

✳✳✳✳

The brisk air tampered against Halle's lips and skin. A shadow figure crossed paths in front of her. Even though her heart was racing she was not frightened. The height and shape gave it away.

"Antonio?"

3

Save yourself

His eyes were the first to be revealed by the street lamps.

His glare could kill "What are you doing out here so late?"

"I had to get out. I thought you were staying at the condo tonight, that's why we all had to leave? Plus I thought you weren't going to be here till later?" she responded

He ignored all the questions "Where are the others?"

"Landry room."

Antonio looked beyond the darkness "Don't tell anybody that you saw me." his shadow faded into the mist

Halle stood frozen, the fear finally was catching up to her. She would never admit that she was afraid of Antonio but sometimes his actions couldn't help but make you fearful.

It was almost two in the morning and the neighborhood was quiet. It was around that time that the cops came out of hiding and all the night ants were off the streets. The Carry on Circle's condo was across the way from Antonio's family's condo. They would pass it every time they would be going home. The laundry room was too far to turn back to so it was closer to go home.

Approaching the stairs Halle could see that Mendoza's condo was lit up like a disco ball. Every single light was on in that house; compared to theirs where you could barely see your hand in front of you.

Something felt off.

As Halle approached closer she heard the sound of a car door lock. Quickly she hid behind a prickly bush as a familiar woman passed by and up the stairs to the condo.

"Jesus Christ Gabreil. Do you have to have every light on in this house?! How is anyone supposed to get any sleep." Maria exclaimed as she threw her keys in the dish

Gabreil, Antonio's dad, sat barely alive on the couch with the muted TV in front of him.

Marcos came out from the other room with a cigarette in his mouth.

"You better not have been smoking with my baby in that room."

He waved the cigarette in her face "Relax chica he's sound asleep and it's not even lit yet."

The condo was a two bedroom and one bath complex. One of the rooms was occupied by the baby and parents while the second bedroom was Gabreils. Even though he spent most of his nights passed out on the couch. Marcos was sober most of the time to be the guard for this place. Nobody besides the immediate Carry on Circle knew this was the Mendoza residence. While the Carry on Circle's place was widely known...the Mendoza's condo could serve as a hiding spot. This condo was minimal but has slightly more furniture than the Carry on Circle. Unfortunately not a crumb of food though.

Gabriel jolted awake and shouted "Who's in my house!"

Marcos grabbed the lighter from the table and joined him on the couch "Go back to sleep old man. Take another pill to hold you over till morning."

He groaned "Nah i'm up."

Maria came back into the living room with her baby in her arms "How could you be with all the lights on. I passed by the Carry on Circle house and it's almost eerie. Then you look over to ours and you can see everything a mile away."

"Just be glad Gabriel wasn't walking around in his underwear." Marcos laughed

Maria didn't laugh but instead had a stern look on her face "Where is Antonio."

Marcos stuttered as he tried to turn to his uncle. "He- he-"

She sat the baby down "HE SHOULD be home by now..."

Marcos lied through his teeth "Him and Tricky are over at the other condo!"

"Without any lights on?"

"Errr." Marcos replied

"So if I go over there right now I'll find him asleep."

Marcos hesitated

Maria put the baby back in the crib then stormed out.

Halle looked both ways then proceeded to get out of the bush with caution. Just then a door slammed

"Maria, wait!" Marcos called out

Halle hurled back into the bush as she watched Maria race over to their condo with Marcos chasing after her.

Uh oh she thought

"Well what if they aren't there?" he yelled

Maria whipped her head around and shushed "Would you be quiet. It is the middle of the night."

She jingled her keys as they took one step at a time up the stairs.

Halle crept behind them and hid at the bottom of the staircase

As Maria slowly turned the handle, Marcos' heart beated out of his ears.

The door swung open and to no surprise the apartment was pitch black.

Maria proceeded with caution because you never know who could be hiding out in here. She headed straight for the bedroom.

She grunted, "What did I say?!" and pushed past Marcos

Halle peaked through the openings between the stairs to see Maria's angry steps descending.

Marcos remained in the dark room "Primo me das de infarto" he whispered to himself with his hand on his heart

The coast was clear as she watched Marcos follow behind like a bad dog. She sighed a relief and tip-toed up the stairs.

She breathed in the smell of fumes covered up with air freshener. This might be the best night's sleep she's gotten in a long time. Finally a night where she could have the big bed and not some paper thin foam mattress on the floor. She shut the world problems behind her as she locked the door.

The Mendoza Apartment

Maria sat with her head in her palms on the cigarette stained couch.

Gabriel, who drifted in and out of sleep, paid no attention to her.

Marcos sat in a nearby chair, silent

In and out of weeps, Maria got some form of a sentence out "It's just *sniff* not fair. I work 12 hour days at a ghetto clinic just to get by paying our bills. If I knew I was going to be a single parent I would have gotten out of this shit hole. *sniff* Antonio doesnt even care enough to see his own son to where he can just disappear without telling anyone."

Marcos lit another cigarette "Sometimes things aren't meant to be."

Maria glared at him through her teary eyes "Meant to be?! I never cry about anything but I can't take this anymore. For once I would love to do something as a family that doesn't get interrupted by drugs."

"I mean he does a lot for you. He runs an entire corporation who would kill for you two. AND he provides you with a roof over your head. Where would you be without him." Marcos replied

She mumbled "Somewhere nicer than this." then raised her voice "How would you feel if you saw your highschool sweetheart an hour a day in the middle of the night, that is if it's a good day. And that you have a child together! I don't and will never want to be a part of the Carry on Circle so I don't know why you guys are always trying to tie me to it."

Marcos shrugged and went into the kitchen

Maria wiped her tears and held her head in her palms. An anger came over her once she noticed Marcos was no longer next to her. She looked to the kitchen then snuck into her room, locking the door behind her. Pulling her flip phone out of her jacket pocket then quickly began dialing.

Anxiety was high as the phone rang. Her heartbeat increased with every ring. Some kind of life had to be on the other side. Everything suddenly stopped when a voice replied *"you've reached the voicemail box of Scott and Beth Bounty. Any information offered can be eligible for cash compensation and may be anonymous. If you choose to leave your name and number we will get back to you as soon as possible. Thank you!"*

The phone beeped and the spotlight was on. Maria took a deep breath. With a shaky voice she proceeded "Hello I would like to remain anonymous because this could end up being dangerous for my son and I. I'm aware that Antonio Mendoza is wanted and we have all been protecting him for too long. But I have reason to believe he's on the run again. Do Whatever it takes to catch him. Hurt whoever you need to...this family is already broken enough."

...if you are satisfied with your message you may now hang up or press one to edit

"No! No! I guess that'll be enough."

A faint baby whimper came from the crib in the dark room. She turned on the table lamp to see a smiling baby just opening his eyes to the world.

"We can't live like this." She whispered to herself

Poking her head in the hallway. First to the living room to find Gabriel still on the couch then Marcos in the other bedroom sound asleep with a cigarette still barely lit in the ashtray next to him.

Maria tiptoed back in her room and darted to the closet. All the way hidden on the top shelf was an emergency go bag. She never thought she would have to use this but if the day came it would be for Antonio's favor. This time it was to save herself. Tugging on the strap caused a little box to fall that the bag was hidden behind.

Maria bent down to meet the fallen box. All the memories of the past 14 years came flooding back.

That first day meeting at the courthouse when they were just 16 till this very moment. The hospital bracelet of their baby's birth right next to Antonio's overdose. The lighters they painted together when Antonio tried to be sober and things actually seemed okay. The pictures of the past ten years.

Tears uncontrollably rolled down her cheeks. The box stopped around 4 years ago when the good memories stopped. She looked at the baby then back at the box. This was the closure she needed to get out.

Without looking back and her whole life was in her arms; she shut the door behind her.

4

The Calm Before the Storm

Halle rolled over to the empty side of the bed. She rubbed her eyes to get a better perception of the sounds around her. The dark sky was still present through the curtains but dawn approached quickly.

Halle cautiously opened the front door. She gasped "Maria?! You scared the bejesus out of me. What are you doing here?"

"I'm coming to say goodbye."

Halle replied with a puzzled look

"I think this is the calm before the storm and God is telling me I need to leave now. I can't believe I'm 30 and starting my life over. And I feel bad this little one will grow up to never know his father but I would rather welcome somebody new in than have him be raised by an active addict."

Halle's jaw fell open

"You can't tell anyone I'm leaving though. I also recommend getting out yourself so you don't get caught up in anything. At least while you still can."

"Where are you going to go?"

"The women's shelter at least until I can get back on my feet. My *own* feet and not having to support everybody else's because I thought we were family. You can't tell anybody you saw me or where I'm going! It can be life threatening if you do."

Halle nodded and went in for a hug "I'll miss you and I wish you the best."

Halle made the long walk over to the laundry room in search of bringing her friends home. Everything Maria said replayed through her mind. Why was she leaving so abruptly? Why was she telling me to get out while I still can?

The sun warmed the path as the cold dreary night phased out.

Halle stood in the doorway to see only Brynn asleep on some towels. She bent down to check her pulse then slowly shook her awake.

Brynn rubbed her dry eyes and talked through her chapped lips "Where did everybody go?"

"That's what I was going to ask you?!" She helped her off the floor "Come on let's go back to the apartment to get you cleaned up."

Brynn stumbled one foot in front of the other up the stairs. Coffee trickled down into the stained mug with faint shower noises coming from the only bathroom.

Halle slid one mug over to Brynn as she joined her at the counter.

She shook the water off her short hair "Ahh this is good. I feel much better. I got into a competition with Zed claiming I could out smoke him...that was a mistake."

Halle rolled her eyes "Brynn sweetie smoking weed is their profession."

Brynn giggled "I know but I thought I could do it. I faintly remember them saying they were heading out to somebody's house but I was long gone before then."

Halle sipped from her mug "I think we should all be staying together. Something is going on right now and I'm not sure what to do."

"What do you mean?!"

"Well this morning Maria came to say goodbye. I couldn't really understand what she was saying but she was saying I should leave before shit hits the fan."

Brynn pondered "I don't understand."

"Now that everyone has disappeared too, I'm thinking maybe she told them the same thing too."

Just then...

The door swung open and a strong stench of marijuana wafted in. Zay and Zed marched in behind the smell.

Halle jumped up "Where the hell have you guys been?!"

"Relax girl, we were over at one of our homies' houses." Zed replied

"And you just left Brynn in the laundry room?"

"Halle believe us she was not moving. We were going to take her but she was damn near lifeless when we were heading out." Zay added

"How responsible. We are family and we can't be split up so if one person goes then we are all going."

The two exchanged looks

"What's she goin on about?" Zay said

Zed shrugged "Ion know man. It's always something."

"Wait, you mean Maria didn't talk to you?"

The two shook their heads

Halle was just about to open her mouth but immediately after the landline rang

Zay motioned for her to answer it

...Hello this is a prepaid call from Los Campos Detention Center from...Kaydon Cross...If you would like to accept press or say 5

Halle froze holding the phone up to her ear. Her heart raced as she confirmed the number

...by confirming you consent to being monitored and recorded

"Hello? Who is there?" Kaydon said frantically

She sighed "Kaydon what did you do?!"

"Oh good Halle. Okay they are keeping me in here for the weekend but I think I can get out on bail Monday if I can come up with the money. I don't have a lot of time to chat but you gotta help me."

"How much is bail?"

"1,000. It's small but I got the money in my stash at the house."

"Yeah I'll see what I can do." she mumbled

"Okay thank you! I only have 30 more seconds left to talk so I'll keep you updated. Don't let me down, Halle."

She left the phone to her ear for a moment listening to the disconnected line. Slowly putting the phone back on the wall she looked at everyone one by one.

"What about Maria?" Zay asked

"No wait, who was that?" Zed asked too

"Well...that was Kaydon...calling from jail..."

You could hear a pin drop

"What did he do?" Zay responded

"He didn't have time to say but he said he needs bail money before the weekend is over."

"Bruh actually? The jail is all the way in the very very North of Los Campos. It'll take like an hour to get there." Zay stated

"He said he has the money. Now we just gotta find a way to give it to him." Halle said

"Well none of us drive...legally...so we will have to rely on Maria to go for us." Zed replied

"Yeah about that..."

"What?"

"Maria has left with the baby. She was telling me I should get out before it's too late too."

"Well did she say her reasoning?" Zay said

"No but now that I think about it, last night I ran into Antonio and he made me swear to deny I ever saw him."

"I thought the whole reason we had to leave WAS BECAUSE him and Tricky were staying here."

"I never saw Tricky and as far as I know he was never here!"

Zay sat down on the couch "So let me get this straight. Maria is gone, Antonio is in hiding, and Tricky is nowhere to be found. The way it sounds to me is that our ring leaders are on the run and left us to take the blame. Like we are already one down!"

"Oh hell no. What happened to loyalty in our blood? I'm certainly not taking the fall for someone who is trying to plant us in the line of blame." Zed shouted

"Are you saying we run too? We aren't wanted though." Halle voiced

"WAIT!? Kaydon is in jail?!"

"Oh my god Brynn keep up." Zed stated

Zay continued "At this point I don't even know if we can trust who's left in the Mendoza family."

"What about Marcos?" Halle suggested

Zay Laughed "I think he's a spy in my opinion but you seem to have a good foundation with him."

"I say we pay a little visit over to the Mendoza apartment and play dumb to see what they know."

The group noded at Halle's response

Meanwhile at the Mendoza residence...

"Uh oh-" Marcos gasped as he looked out the window

"WHAT what!" Gabriel exclaimed

"Okay maybe i'm just being paranoid but two all blacked out big SUVs just pulled into the parking lot and they're all decked out in bullet proof vests and i can see the sun reflecting off their badges."

"No no no how do they know we were here." Gabriel panicked and reached for his pill bottle

"We don't know if they are here for us or not. We act casual and say we don't know anything."

"Someone had to have ratted us out that we were here because nobody knew about us besides the immediate Carry on Circle."

"Uncle Gabreil relax. With Antonio being on the run and Maria is randomly missing. I'm sure somebody made somebody mad and now our butts are at stake."

"We aren't going to let that happen though because we haven't done anything besides protect our family."

"Correct. I'm going to go talk to Carry on Circle and hopefully stay out of their sight."

"Marcos wait!" Gabriel called out to him as he opened the front door "don't be afraid to throw anyone in their path to distract them from us."

Marcos nodded and made his way down the stairs. He weaved in and out of the hidden walkways and stayed out of plain sight.

Gabriel watched from the window as they surrounded a blacked out truck with no plates.

Marcos stood around the corner peeking through the bushes. His heart raced. Just as he turned his back to head over to the Carry on Circle residence he heard a yell.

...*"HEY! Guy in the hat."*

Oh god oh god how did they even see me Marcos thought to himself

His heart raced as they approached closer

"Hey man we just got a couple questions for anyone we see walking the streets. He extended a hand shake then showed his badge "My name is Dewy and this is my sister Grace. We are bounty hunters and we have reason to believe a fugitive is hiding out here."

Marcos didn't say anything and slightly nodded

Grace handed him a wanted poster "Do you recognize this man?"

Marcos' eyes widened. He had to shake his head. His voice was quaky but he muttered "Nope, never seen him around here."

"Do you know who's blacked out tint vehicle with no plates belongs to out in the lot?" Grace asked

Just as Marcos thought he was in the clear he felt his heart drop again "Yes...that's my truck. Is there an issue?"

"Well not yet anyways. We have reason to believe the fugitive drives cars with your same description and switches them out with family members."

Uh oh Marcos thought

"Just to confirm your identity we will need to see your license and registration to confirm the car is yours." Grace added on

"It's- it's upstairs in my apartment." Marcos said

"We found the owner of the truck!" Dewy shared on the radio "Alright man come over and talk to my folks. If you truly don't know this guy then they'll let you walk but if you do then we are going to have to ask more questions."

Putting one foot in front of the other Marcos felt his whole world becoming blurry around him. Each foot step was like a loud stomp in his ear drums. All he could think about was his cover being blown. Staying calm and collected was the key to getting out of this.

The Bountys introduced themselves, Scott and Beth, then their second son, Justin. Marcos still remained unnamed.

Marcos listened closely to how Scott explained the situation

..."So if you could just show us some identification to the car to prove it's yours then we will be on our way."

In hopes to get some kind of game plan out of this. Everything they knew Marcos needed to be a step ahead to get himself out of this mess.

"Everything is upstairs. My license and keys I can run up there and go get it for you."

"Oh we can come with you then." Justin stated

Marcos hesitated and turned his neck to the apartment right behind them. The outline of Gabriel was still in the window.

"If you don't let us come with you then it'll look like you're hiding something and you wouldn't want that...right?" Beth said

"Yes! That should be fine." Marcos replied

I hope you're prepared Tio he thought as the agents followed behind him up the stairs

Gabriel's eyes were like burning hot lasers on Marcos when everyone filed inside.

As Marcos dug in his drawer to find his wallet he heard Gabriel only speaking Spanish from the other room.

He laughed "What a con artist he is. No wonder his son is wanted."

Entering the living room again Marcos handed his wallet over to Beth just to notice Grace looking at the photos.

"Who are all the people in these photos because none of them really look like you?" she asked

"Those are my Tios kids, so my cousins."

Marcos bit his nails as Beth slowly pulled his ID out of his wallet.

"Marcos MENDOZA?!" Beth exclaimed

5

Running, Running, Running

"WHERE IS YOUR SON?! And how about your daughter?! Changing her number then pi cking up and moving while she is still listed as the cosigner that could be a crime too you know. You better start calling and get one of them on the phone!"

Gabriel's legs began to shake and he started to dry heave.

"Okay okay sit him down. He's too old to be under this stress." Marcos ordered

Scott followed him to the couch "Where is your son brotha?! You better find him and get him here because we aren't playing around!"

Gabriel stuttered over his words "I- I don't know- where any of my kids are"

Dewy shook his head at Marcos "You said you had no idea who this man was but it turns out you're related to him."

An hour of back and forth went by when Beth finally stated "Okay while you guys figure this out Marcos is going to take me and Grace back downstairs to look in this car. Hopefully by then Gabriel will have his story straight."

Marcos held his breath when Grace and Beth looked inside the car. Deep down he knew their tracks were covered but he never knew if there was about to be an oopsie with something left out.

"At least you can prove this car is yours and it wasn't stolen. I'm sure you guys are familiar with that." Beth said

Marcos had a sigh of relief when he was given the all clear

"Beth, wait before we go back up the stairs I need to know what's going on."

She motioned to the stairs to take a seat "So what's going on this family is in a lot of trouble. Antonio is putting a lot of his loved ones in danger because a lot of people rely on him. If he goes away then people might start coming after you so it's best that he does go away so you guys can move on."

"I've been dealing with this since I was 14 and Antonio and I started becoming close. That's my cousin though I love him."

"I know you do and I can guarantee what he's doing isn't showing he loves you guys back. Right now you guys are playing the victim and denying you're involved but if we find out any of the family is involved then it's going to be all bad."

Grace added on "And once we get Antonio off the street then all your family problems stemming from him will be gone."

"I don't know anything though!"

Just then they heard yelling coming from upstairs

"What is going on in here?!" Beth exclaimed

"Gabriel is getting high right in front of us!"

Marcos shook his head

"I have paperwork, I swear." Gabriel shouted "Marcos get me my prescription receipt."

Marcos' hands shook as he handed it over to Scott. This piece of paper laid heavy on his conscience.

Just a few minutes later it was quiet. Almost too quiet with the bounties being gone.

Gabriel sighed in relief "I can't believe they bought it."

"And what are you going to do when Antonio is locked up and he can't write you those prescriptions anymore."

"Hey! Don't talk like that. From now on we deny deny deny anything Antonio could be a suspect of. We will never admit to anything he has done even if it's a proven fact. At this point I'm ready to throw Carry on Circle under the bus so it distracts them from us. By then it'll buy us some time to get out of this situation."

"Don't talk like that."

"Marcos you don't get it. These people that belong to the Carry on Circle arent family like we are. They aren't blood so they will go down before we do as long as I have control."

"I'll be back." Marcos said as he shut the door behind him

The sun had just started to set as Marcos made the walk over to the Carry on Circle apartment. He knew that with all of this the only thing he could do was warn the others. This was the last opportunity to show that he cared before Gabriel did something that would affect all of them.

He took a deep breath before knocking on the door.

Halle answered with a smile "Since when do you knock weirdo."

She noticed immediately something was wrong by Marcos expression

Marcos tried to look inside "Who is all here?"

"Me, Zay, Zed, and Brynn. Everyone headed out for the night so it's just us for now."

"Perfect, can I come in?"

Halle raised an eyebrow and stood to the side for him to enter

"Yo Marcos, where is your cousin brotha." Zay asked

Marcos hesitated

"Yeah if he is on the run again why didn't he let us know."

"Well I'm glad you guys already know."

"Are you serious?! He's actually on the run again." Halle scoffed

"There have been a lot of things going on and we are all in big trouble." Marcos said

"When was the last time you saw him?" Zed asked

"He was here last night talking to Gabriel and I about his plan. He left before Maria got home but you guys have to swear not to say anything. Scott and Beth Bounty just left our house with their whole crew so Gabriel and I are coming up with a story to try and protect us all."

"No way you're kidding." Halle replied

"THEY WERE HERE?!" Brynn exclaimed "We are all doomed."

"Not necessarily that's why we are trying to come up with a plan but that's also why I wanted to come talk to you guys. I don't know what my tio is going to say or do but he sounds like he is set in stone on protecting his family."

"But we are considered family right?" Halle asked

Marcos paused "That's how it should be but you guys aren't blood in his eyes."

"I told you there was something shady about him that I didn't trust!" Halle said

"After everything we have done for him and his family yet he still sees us as pawns." Zay said in between puffs of smoke

"I just wanted to warn you guys on what's been going on."

"Did you hear Kaydon is in jail?" Halle responded

Marcos hook his head

Zed added on "Yup we are one man down so when it rains it pours right."

"We aint going to be next though." Zay said

"Keep us updated alright" said Halle

"Of course. I'll do everything I can because in my eyes you guys are family." Marcos stated as he showed himself out

"I can tell you one thing. I don't wanna stick around to find out." Zay told

"Me neither, I think we need to get out of sight...tonight." Halle mentioned

"I never thought we would be on the run too." Zed laughed

Halle explained "On the bright side we aren't wanted so we just need to lay low until this all blows over then we can either move on or go back to our current lives."

"And we know that will only happen when Antonio and Tricky are in jail. Speaking of that, have we heard anything from Tricky?" Zed asked

Zay shook his head "At this point I think him and Antonio have split or we would have heard they are running together."

"Last thing I heard from Tricky is he is doing pretty good. He has just been struggling with going to court and that's what has been biting him in the ass." Halle added

"I still can't believe Kaydon is in jail." Brynn said

Halle gasped "Uh oh that's right. We would have to get the money to him by tomorrow and it probably wouldn't be a good idea to go anywhere near law enforcement."

"And if we run and they raid our house then we WILL be wanted." Zay stated

"It's a lose lose situation but we just have to decide what will be best for us." Zed added

"Our pictures are on so many IDs so no matter how much evidence we destroy it'll be difficult to make sure we don't miss anything." Halle said

Zay responded "Maybe that's it. We leave it and just get the hell out of dodge. Maybe Gabriel will keep everything hush hush and we won't even get brought into this."

The group grabbed as many backpacks as they could and fit as much stuff as they could into them. They worked as quickly but as quietly as they could. They had to make it seem like everything was as normal as possible. It worked perfectly that it was getting dark out too so that way they could move with the shadows.

No notes, no goodbye, just disappearing into the night.

The Carry on Circle left everything just how it was but only grabbed the essentials. They had to make it seem like they were coming back even if they never did.

Zay and Zed told the girls they could stay at their friends house down the street for a night then after that they were on their own.

Their friends were straight up trappers. It helped that they have all met before so the girls weren't just strangers in a trap home.

There were about twenty people crammed into this little town house with furniture replaced with drugs, weapons, and money.

If you thought the Carry on Circle apartment was bad...this home was a hundred times grimer and **illegal.**

Zay and Zed's friends actually came into play a lot when helping them plan their escape. These people were true criminals who hid in plain sight. They never had to worry about getting caught up because people respected them too much.

One of the guys drew out a map with motels and resources along the way with the final destination being a ranch deep past the county line of Los Campos.

"Woah I never knew about this and I feel like I knew a lot of the hiding spots." Halle said

One of the Trappers traced the route with a knife "This place could get you killed if you do something stupid. You have ex 19th West members hiding out here, criminals on the run, and to your surprise you might find Antonio and Tricky here."

Another Trapper added on "You should head out tonight and move in the dark. A lot of these motels won't ask questions because they are doing some shady shit too.

The first Trapper said "We can give you a lift there but after that we aren't involved."

The second Trapper said "The end goal is to avoid going to jail and not taking people down with you."

The Carry on Circle nodded and shook hands with the two trappers.

The car ride was quiet and casual to avoid drawing any attention to themselves. It was about 20 minutes outside the East Side to get to their first destination. Eventually they pulled up to a semi empty parking lot with a big neon sign in the front that said **BoomTown Motel**

"Good luck." The driver said as the two trappers drove away

"You know I don't even think I know their names." Halle said to Zay and Zed

"Good they probably wanna keep it like that." Zay replied

"How did you even meet them?" she asked

Zed laughed "The universe works in mysterious ways but those two guys are some of the most badasses we have ever met."

"For real it would suck to lose them." Zay added

"Hey!" Brynn exclaimed

"What?!" The group jumped together

"Nothing, I just haven't said anything for a while." she laughed

Zay and Zed looked to Halle

"Did we have to bring her?" Zed rolled his eyes

"Um yes because she can be smart when she wants to AND because we aren't leaving anyone behind!"

Zay laughed, "My money is on her getting arrested first."

Halle opened the lobby door for everyone. "Actually Kaydon was the first to get arrested."

6
Down a man

"So how are things going with you guys?"
Marcos asked

Halle looked at her friends who were still
sleeping "So far so good. We got in kind of late last
night so I think we are just going to chill here for
the day, maybe go out and get some essentials."

The sound of knocking came through the
phone

"Who's at your house?" She asked

"I don't know but what worries me a little
bit. Ever since we got a visit from the bounty
hunters yesterday, we have all been on high alert."

"Has anyone even noticed we are missing?"

"The conversation hasn't gotten to big yet-"

"Marcos, can you answer the dang door!"
Gabriel shouted from the other room

"Halle I got to-"

She replied instantly "it's okay I totally
understand. Besides we have prepaid minutes that
we have to save so we will talk soon"

The knocking became more intense as the longer Marcos waited to open the door. His hand hovered over the lock as Gabriel came out in baggy clothes from the other room.

"Remember what we talked about." He mumbled

Marcos opened the door with a plastered smile still with the phone in his hand

"Took you long enough." Scott stated

Marcos' heart skipped a beat each time one of the Bounty's walked through their doorway; soon enough he's going to have to start taking Gabriel's "medication".

His voice cracked "coFee anyone?"

They looked over to their stained coffee maker

"No thank you and I don't think you should have any either. It'll make you more anxious than you already are." Beth replied

Grace observed his behavior "Is there any reason why you are so nervous? We are just here to chat."

Marcos gulped as Scott grabbed the seat directly in front of Gabriel.

Life came from one of the two beds.

"Good morning sunshine." Halle laughed

Brynn's hair stood up in all different directions "I feel like I got run over by a truck."

"Maybe you shouldn't have drank that much mysterious liquid on our way here from the Trappers."

Brynn rolled her eyes and fell back into the pillow

An unknown number pinged the burner phone. Halle took a cautious step in answering this call. There was no guarantee who was on the other line but something told her she would be surprised.

"Hello? Who is this?" she answered

"Halle? Oh thank god. Where have you guys been!" a familiar voice asked

"Antonio?" she whispered into the phone

"Yes yes its me-"

"One second let me go outside."

She let the door fall behind her, sneaking out quiet as a mouse. "Okay go."

"Where are you guys?!"

"In a disclosed location. I should be asking you the same thing. Where have *YOU* been and where are you calling from? Also how did you get this number?"

"I am calling from a pay phone on the South side but I'm not staying here for long. I am going back to...actually I can't tell you I don't know who's listening. How is everything at home?"

Halle paused "Uh- I just said we are in a disclosed location because we had to leave rapidly. Marcos didn't tell you which I'm assuming how you got this number. We need help Antonio, can we please meet up?"

"I just need to know if you've told anyone you saw me a couple nights ago."

"No I haven't told anyone? But you still haven't answered my past five questions."

"We can talk about it when I see you next."

"And when will that be because we might not make it." she whispered into the phone "We are heading to this ranch outside of Los Campos.."

Antonio was quiet for a second

"Hello?" Halle said again

"You can't go there! Where would you even get an idea about that?"

"Why not? It seems like our only option till the problems with you blow over."

He answered rapidly, "We will talk soon."

Halle pulled the phone away from her ear "That bastard."

"Hey where did you go?" Zay asked as he sat up in bed

Halle had a blank expression on her face "I just needed some fresh air."

"Oh okay. I was thinking today, if we can find a ride, we go down to the park and try to make some money. Plus we can hang out with the people we haven't seen in a while."

"I mean if that's what you guys wanna do?"

Zay looked to Zed who was still passed out and to Brynn who had fallen back asleep.

A violent buzzing went off in Halle's hand. This time a familiar number was calling but no answer came from Halle.

I'm sorry Kaydon, I can't deal with this right now. She thought

"Aren't you going to answer that?" he asked

Halle looked down at the phone one more time then turned it off "No it's probably just a telemarketer. Yeah, let's do something today. It's been a while since we've done anything fun."

✷✷✷✷

Marcos overheard everything Gabriel was telling Scott and felt his stomach sink. Gabriel would say anything and everything to get his family out of trouble. Anything Antonio has done he will place the blame and say someone else did it. The Carry on Circle brings drugs into the city...partially true. The Carry on Circle worships Antonio till the end to where they just distribute it for him. Antonio is actually the one who brings all the drugs in.

One of his clients needs a new shotgun but can't risk buying one legally. Someone is right there scratching the serial number off in the closet. And of course the biggest thing of it all...the identity circle. One man distributing enough drugs, money, and weapons to supply a whole city with the help of hundreds whose livelihoods depend on this one man.

Marcos knew the second the Bounty's step foot into this apartment the Carry on Circle was over. Everything Antonio has built over the years will be gone in an instant. He didn't know who would be in this apartment when they walked in but whoever is in there is about to be done for. He just hoped it wasn't any of the people he called family.

All this circled around in his head as they stopped in their tracks waiting for the rest of the crew. He never thought he would see the day where he watched all his friends get arrested in front of him while he stood as a bystander.

He couldn't bear to poke his head in to see if it was anyone he knew or was close with.

A few minutes later after the all clear Gabriel came over and had no problem entering the apartment.

Hours went by as the bounty hunters questioned the randoms inside the house.

Marcos' hands could barely hold a cigarette as he waited at the bottom of the stairs. All the what if possibilities came through one by one as the rumbles up stairs continued. Periodically one of the bounty hunters would come down and check on him.

"You still doing okay out here?" Dewy asked

Marcos released a cloud of smoke

"Are you sure you don't wanna come inside? This could be the last time you see this place...or claim anything that's yours before the police find it."

Marcos felt his heart drop "What do you mean by that?"

Dewy made his way down the stairs "I'm just saying you were close with these people so I'd assume you've been over here. Especially because our cousin's name is on the lease. You want to do the right thing, right?"

Marcos nodded

"Don't let what your uncle is saying get in the way of getting yourself out of trouble. We are here to make everything right and help people along the way. I know my parents can be intimidating but when everything is settled they become the biggest softies. You just have to be honest with us."

Marcos felt his soul begin to crack within him.

"I'll give you some time to think if you need it-" Dewy said

"No wait." Marcos called out "It's too late to try and protect them any longer. It's hard because I still have so much love for them but what's done is done. I'm ready to be honest with what the Carry on Circle is and the truth behind Antonio. No more lies."

✳✳✳✳

Halle waved goodbye to their driver "I hate to say it but it was nice socializing with everyone we haven't seen in a while."

"Well I'm glad you ended up having fun even though you were looking over your shoulder the entire time." Zay laughed

"I was concerned for Brynn because she's the biggest target since she's actually done time before, out of all of us."

Zay responded "Maybe that's because she's not all there."

"Excuse me, I'm standing right here! Plus getting arrested for public intoxication and spending 3 hours in booking but getting released IS NOT DOING TIME! "

"You know I love you but it's the truth. Anyways Halle, didn't that make you miss the adrenaline in the streets. Especially being at the top." he said as he handed the money off to Zed

"If anything it made me feel bad for those poor souls who are at the bottom of the chain. I see things differently than you guys do." Just then the buzzing of their burner phone shook the dresser

Zed swiped it

"Hey! Let me see it!" Halle exclaimed

Zed waved the phone around "This number has been calling all day! What are you hiding? "Wait Halle weren't we supposed to get Kaydon his money today?"

She gulped and picked up the burner that rang a second time "Crap, Kaydon's calling again."

"Ignore it." Zay replied

"I can't, we've already been ignoring him all day and it's almost dusk."

"Just tell him something came up and we couldn't bail him out."

"I mean you're not wrong."

"It only rings so many times you gotta make your decision soon." Zed added

"I wanna talk to him!" Brynn exclaimed

...*Hello this is a prepaid call from Los Campos Detention Center from...Kaydon Cross...If you would like to accept press or say 5*

"Hey are you guys almost here? Time is ticking and I was supposed to be out hours ago?"

Halle hesitated "Kaydon, I'm sorry but you have to stay in there."

There was a silence on the other line then a soft stern voice "What do you mean I have to stay in here..."

"Something came up to where we can't go anywhere near authorities let alone a jail."

"You're kidding right. What happened when you were promising me that you were giving me MY MONEY today!"

"Well we weren't wanted then- Plus we are on the outskirts of Los Campos. No where near the North side."

"Jesus christ." Kaydon scoffed "You know I've been pissed at you guys before but never this bad. I am completely done with you,The Carry on Circle and Antonio. You all are a bunch of selfish rats who don't think about anybody except themselves. I risked everything being the backbone of this group and of course was the one to get wrapped first. I got wrapped DOING YOUR GUYS DIRTY WORK. Now I'm facing an even bigger investigation when they find out more people are involved with these IDs. It won't just be a misdemeanor in the end and you guys are okay with that. You guys won't survive without me and I really want to see you try!"

"Kaydon im so sorry please try and understand-"

He interrupted, "Does Antonio even know I'm locked up?"

Halle replied "I doubt it but honestly he has so much going on right now so I don't think he really cares."

A frustrated sigh came from the other line "Typical."

"Kaydon..." Halle whispered but she was only talking to a dead line

She turned to her friends "Well we are officially down a man."

"You know if I ever get locked up, which will never happen, I'm going to start a money ring inside there so I would have to keep you guys around." Zay laughed with a joint in his mouth

"You would be committing a crime while doing time for another crime?" Halle said

"Not exactly because with the new money transferring websites that may or may not be legal yet; it's going to be allowed in prisons." Zay replied

Halle chuckled, "Right...you just keep telling yourself that."

7
The Chase

"I'm glad that's over with." Gabriel said as he opened the pill bottle "I felt the organs start to rattle within me. I was so nervous."

Marcos did not have a reply

"I'm surprised none of the main Carry on Circle members were there."

Gabriel looked at his nephew with a confused look on why he wasn't responding.

He mumbled "I heard you tell Scott that they always need things from us yet you're the one always offering to help them. The immediate members of the Carry on Circle have never asked for anything from us nor have they taken anything."

"Why are you protecting them so hard? You're going to end up going down with them."

"That's what I fear the most."

"But nothing in that apartment was yours right?" Gabriel asked

Marcos hesitated

Gabriel put his hand over his eyes

Quick to defend, Marcos said "Just one ID and that could easily have been lost."

"How could you be so stupid!" Gabriel shouted

"Tio-"

Gabriel continued "You realize we had a good thing going. They think I'm too old to know what's going on or just wrapped up in dope. They're relying on you for all the information but now they have something on you so you're even more of a target."

Marcos looked him dead in the eyes "If they would have found something of mine then there would be cops surrounding our home right now and I would be long gone. The ID is the least of my worries. The second Scott finds out we have met before my life is over. He will find any and every way to throw me in jail and leave me there to rot."

"We all make big mistakes and *that one* wasn't entirely your fault."

"Antonio and I were there and we did nothing. We let him die on us because we were too afraid of the consequences and I've had to live with that ever since. To me that is the biggest punishment."

Gabriel pondered "We will get ourselves out of this; but just for that you're going to make the dreaded call to Antonio to tell him what is going on. Do it as soon as possible! And sobrino, do not throw me under the bus or you'll regret it."

Marcos reached for his pack of cigarettes, his white "good luck" lighter, and phone. He took a deep breath as the brisk air hit his lips. He could barely keep his fingers still to dial the number.

"Don't pick up, don't pick up..."

"Hello, who is this?"

Marcos felt like he was punched in the gut "H- hi is Antonio there?"

"Can I ask who's calling and from where?"

Marcos cleared his throat "Zorro. And from Gabriel's house."

There was a silence on the other line

"Hello primo? What's going on?"

"Antonio! Did you already hear?"

"No? God damn it hear what? I'm asking what happened because I told you to only call the ranch when it's an emergency and that we will talk when I call you. So let me ask again, what is going on?"

Marcos took a deep breath "The bounty hunters found out about the Carry on Circle and raided the house today. 12 came to confiscate everything and made eight arrests."

There was a long pause from the other line "Are they looking for me?"

"Yes. and your dad thought revealing the Carry on Circle would create a distraction but now things are spiraling out of control."

"So it was my fucking dad. You know what I was going to start losing it but I don't even care. If all these people are going to go down for me then so mote it be."

"So you don't care if Halle, Zay, Zed, and Brynn go down too?" Marcos asked

"Whoever keeps me out of jail. As long as they dont find me here."

"How is Tricky?"

Antonio's voice trailed off "He's good...most likely. Look, just try and do whatever's necessary to make sure the ops stay off my back. I'm going to get in contact with Salia. I think she's coming back to Los Campos pretty soon."

"Primo I'm sorry." Marcos said

"No, don't apologize. You're doing what's right for the family. Yeah it sucks all my rare guns and everything I sold my soul for to get is now taken but I appreciate everything you're doing to keep me out of jail. I love you primo."

Wow that went better than expected Marcos thought

Antonio looked over to the empty side of the room where Tricky stayed.

I sure hope you are good buddy. He thought

The Boomtown Motel

Zay and Halle lounged on the railing outside their room. Not much was said, just smoke and vibes.

"I can't believe you would choose a cigarette, literally useless nicotine, over marijuana." Zay laughed

Halle took a hit of her cigarette "I refuse to go back to drugs. Everytime we smoke together you tell me this. A cigarette once in a while is okay, especially in a stressful situation. After all, I can't give up smoking altogether when I'm in a family of addicts; I can't be looked at as the lame one." she laughed

Brynn poked her head out of the room "Halle the phone is ringing."

"Why can't you or Zed answer it?" she asked

Brynn's eyes were bright red "Do you think that's a good idea right now."

Halle reached for the phone and put out her cigarette on the concrete.

Before she should even answer there was already screaming on the other line.

"WHAT THE HELL WERE YOU GUYS THINKING! Everything we have worked for EVERYTHING WE SPENT YEARS DOING is now gone! I can't believe you guys let all these people go to jail. And where were you guys when all of this was happening?!"

"Antonio! What is going on!" Halle shouted over him "Only Kaydon has gotten arrested and everything at home should be okay?!"

"NO it's most certainly not. Marcos didn't tell you? The pigs raided the Carry on Circle house."

Halle was at a loss for words. She muttered into the phone "Oh my god Maria was right."

"Maria?! What does Maria have to do with this?" Antonio questioned

"How did she know all of this was going to happen?!'

"WAIT DID MARIA SNITCH?! I trusted her with my life and she goes and betrays me like this!?-"

Halle interrupted "No no no she didn't do anything. I thought you would have found out by now. Antonio, she up and left with your son the night you started to run again."

Antonio paused, "She left me?"

"I'm sorry Antonio, I was shocked when she told me. I don't even think your dad and cousin know. She came to me when she was on her way out in hopes you would be at the apartment."

"Wow- we have been together since we were 16. I guess all of that meant nothing to her. Did she say where she was going?"

Halle hesitated. A part of her didn't believe Antonio was this distraught of Maria's absence. All that could play in her head was Maria begging her not to disclose her location "No she didn't say. I don't think she wanted anyone to see her."

"Anyways back to what happened today. What were you telling me earlier about this location you were going to?"

"Antonio I can't talk for long because we have to make our prepaid minutes last. I can call you from a payphone tomorrow?"

He sighed "Yeah sure that's fine. Now that I know this is going on I have to limit my time out in the world. Tomorrow give me the number to your closest pay phone just so I have it on record. Now just know **the chase is on.**"

"Yeah sure no problem. I'm sorry again Antonio I know this isn't what you wanted to deal with right now..." She turned back to Zay "Deadline. You know I feel bad for Antonio."

"Why? Wasn't he literally just screaming at you and saying something was your fault when it wasn't." Zay stated

"Yeah but-"

"HE IS THE ROOT OF ALL PROBLEMS HALLE!"

"Woah chill. If you feel this way about him, why have you stuck around for so long?"

"Because that's my brother Halle. It's different than you think."

"How? Because as far as I'm concerned we are ALL family. And it just so happens us in this room are the closet with Antonio and Tricky."

Zay inhaled the last bit of smoke "Then why has it gotten to the point where he only comes around when he needs something."

Halle reached for her lighter and popped another cigarette in her mouth. The door closed behind Zay as he went back inside. The cool fresh air was a nice balance between the clouds of smoke. In a way Zay was right. Why was Antonio just coming around when he needed something or when shit was hitting the fan. Also the fact that Tricky was nowhere to be found.

All the good memories with Antonio came flooding back. Back when he used to actually kick it with the Carry on Circle and demonstrated what it meant to be a family.

Now all of that was out the window and Antonio was right...The Chase was On.

8

One Step Ahead

Dewy snuck out the door and down the steps to find Marcos down there.

Marcos turned around with a glossy eye

"Have you had any contact with The Carry on Circle at all?" Dewy asked

"No, not since they ran." Marcos answered

"Well I'm going to tell you this, that you can maybe benefit from it. We got a hot lead from an informant today that says they are on the border of Los Campos. Do you know anywhere that they might be?"

Marcos said "The outskirts of Los Campos lead into farmland. I know there is a janky motel out there and gas stations. About 30 minutes from the South side is a town called Los Gateos which you shouldn't believe everything you see at first glance. They are known for their farming so I don't think they would be there."

"Yeah I've been there. There isn't really much there unless you are a resident. I see you go to great lengths to protect your cousin. Why not The Carry on Circle?" Dewy asked

"They aren't blood." Marcos mumbled

Some time passed and The Bounty's crossed paths with Marcos as he made his way back up to the apartment.

"You didn't say anything did you?" Gabriel asked

"Not about Antonio." Marcos replied

"Because when Dewy was down there talking to you then he comes back and says they got a lead. That's suspicious as hell nephew."

Marcos sighed "At this point I'm tired of this and want it to stop. I will still do anything to protect my family but these people, The Carry on Circle, are making it hell for us."

"Now you're starting to get it." Gabriel said

It was just before midnight. The boys were taking in their last puffs of smoke on the patio while Brynn had been in the bathroom for a while doing god knows what. Halle laid staring up at the ceiling with a blank mind.

We have been hiding out in plain sight for three days and it's been exhausting. When can we safely get into hiding then we won't even have to worry about this...but at the same time is this all worth it. Once we get into hiding we just have to wait for this whole thing to blow over...does it even work like that? I didn't do anything though...besides anything and everything illegal then ran from it...okay maybe I did do something. Antonio promised all of us though that we would never have to do jail time. I guess when things grow so big it's hard to keep your promises. I would ride for any of the people in this room and some outside of here. Would it be reciprocated for me?

Halle's thoughts were interrupted when the bathroom door swung wide open

"HEY GIRL HEY!" Brynn shouted

Just then Zay and Zed were walking back in

"What did she take?" Zay asked

"I was just getting to that...Brynn WHAT ARE YOU ON?!" Halle yelled

Brynn just laughed and flopped down on the bed

"What is that ringing?" Zed said covering his ears

Brynn pulled out a buzzing phone from under her "Take this stupid thing."

Zay laughed, "It wasn't even that loud brudder."

Zed looked in the prescription bottle that they kept their weed in "I think something must have gotten mixed in with it and is messing my mind up."

Zay narrowed his eyes "I smoked the same thing you did? I swear you two are cracking under pressure and Halle and I are the only sane ones here."

"UGH! I missed the call. Huh weird for some reason there is no reception here where I can call back. But it looks like a voicemail was left." Halle held the phone up to her ear...

"...Hey guys it's Marcos not sure why you didn't answer but be on high alert because Scott and Beth just left here and they are heading your way I think. They said they got a hot lead on The Carry on Circle and had to dip. Halle if I was you I would get the hell out of there."

The phone fell out of her hands and it was like slow motion as it hit the ground.

She looked everyone deep in their eyes "Run!"

"WHAT HUH NOW?" Zed exclaimed

Zay rubbed his eyes "What now Halle?"

She swiftly packed up as much stuff as she could into a backpack "Marcos called *inhale* and *exhale* somebody snitched and the bounty hunters are on their way."

There was a silence for a second then Zay and Zed jumped into fight or flight mode.

A panic overcame Halle's voice "Brynn you have to sober up, we need to go now!"

"You know i'm tired of you always bossing me around-" she snarked

Halle raised both eyebrows and without hesitation slapped Brynn across the face "THIS IS NO TIME TO PLAY GAMES!" She looked at Zay and Zed "Don't just stand there. Pick your jaws up off the floor and let's get going."

Taking one last look in their room they quickly shut the door behind them.

"Where are we going to go now?!" Zed asked

"Anywhere we go they'll see us."

Halle looked to some bushes that rounded the corner to the side of the hotel. "Go there, we should be able to watch what's going on."

They crept into a little huddle of overgrown bushes and trees that camouflage them from the lights and eyesight.

Halle was able to see from afar two big black SUVs serving into the parking lot then a man and woman go into the lobby as three others surrounded the building.

She could feel everyone's heart beating in sync as they crouched down.

She whispered "Move a little more in."

"Don't think we won't kick this door in!" shouted Scott

crack

"God Brynn be quiet." Zed whispered

"I'm sorry that there is a branch right here." she rolled her eyes

Headlights shined into the bushes where the Carry on Circle laid. Halle's eyes appeared over the shrubs to see more bodies running to surround the room.

"Guns grab the guns and circle around the back." Scott ordered as the rest of the crew pulled up

"Come on, we need to get out of here! We can sneak out from where they just came from." Zay said

"Just one more minute." Halle mumbled

"Kick it in!" Beth yelled

Halle motioned "Go go now"

Carry on Circle hid in the shadows and dodged through the leaves. They could hear faint yelling from the back. Not knowing where to go now their best option was to hide in plain sight. They escaped this time but the next isn't guaranteed.

They followed the road up to the nearest little gas station where they could hide out until the bounty hunters left.

Halle tried to catch her breath before giving the next directions "We *gasp* will *breathe* hide around back and dodge cameras. Someone goes inside and asks for the bathroom key. While we wait I'll call Marcos to see if he will come pick us up and can take us to the ranch."

The phone blared next to Marcos' ear awakening him from his slumber "Hello who's this?"

"Marcos, thank god. You were right they totally did come here and raid us. We are hiding out in the gas station a little up the street from the motel. Can you please come pick us up and take us to the ranch?"

He paused. Of course he was fed up with the situation but he still felt the need to help.

"Hello Marcos?" She said again

"I can come get you but I can't take you to the ranch. It's too risky going there at night. "

"Then where are we supposed to go?" she asked

Marcos hesitated "being back at home is better than hiding out in a bathroom all night? You can figure it out."

Halle was taken aback "You mean we can't stay with you guys just for a few hours?"

"The bounty hunters have been showing up to our house randomly. We can't take that chance."

"Wow- Remember Marcos we are the ones probably going down for your cousin." Halle said

"Okay alright fine. I will sneak you in while my tio is asleep."

"Thank you!"

"I'll be there in 30." Marcos replied

Marcos carefully grabbed his eyes out of the nightstand drawer and his jacket from the closet. He moved in the dark to avoid any complications. He took one step in front of the other avoiding the creeks in the floor and tiptoed to the door. He stopped in front of Gabriel's room to where he could see a pitch black room through the door crack. He slowly unlocked the door and silently shut it behind him. He wouldn't be in the clear until he was down the road.

Halle turned to Zay and Zed "Marcos said we can stay with him but we have to be out before Gabriel gets up."

"Could this be a trap?" Zay asked

"We don't have a choice. Where are we going to go?" Halle replied

Zed said "Aren't we just starting back at square one?"

Halle shook her head but didn't respond.

At this time Brynn was back and kept dramatically sighing.

Zay and Zed kept exchanging looks but didn't dare say anything.

Zay thought *Oh shit something is about to go down...*

After a couple minutes Halle had enough "Yes Brynn, do you need to say something."

"Actually yes i'm glad you asked-"

Halle interrupted "I don't need the attitude right now. Just share your feelings so we can move on."

She scoffed, "Well. that's disrespectful."

Halle sat there quiet waiting for this to pass over

Brynn kept going "I just don't appreciate how you've been bossing us around this entire time and how you forced us out of our home. Like I don't know who put you in charge of all of us but we should be able to take care of ourselves."

The boys laughed

Zed chimed in "Yeah try taking care of yourself and see how far that gets you."

"I'm not finished." Brynn said

"Well I'm finished listening. Do you understand what's going on? If we would have stayed at The Carry on Circle house then we would all be in jail right now! Don't yell at me for trying to keep you guys safe. Even in this situation all you guys worry about is the next time you can get high." Halle exclaimed

Zay said "Hey don't bring Zed and I into this! We have been following your lead."

Halle ignored him "If you feel I am bossing you around then you can run on your own."

Brynn shouted "We wouldn't be in this mess in the first place if it wasn't because of you!"

Halle yelled back "WHAT?! You're not even making any sense." she held up Brynn's arm "LAY OFF THE DRUGS! Do you not see what it's doing to you? We used to be best friends. We did everything together. It started with an alliance because we were the only girls which brought us closer. It was never me. I ONLY GOT BETTER WITH TIME...you got worse. I don't even recognize the person you are anymore."

Brynn was silent

Headlights shined in through the frosted glass window above the bathroom door.

Zay whispered "Marcos must be here."

Halle picked up her stuff and looked at Brynn who wasn't moving.

"Are you coming with us?" she asked

"I don't know, I thought you guys wanted me out." Brynn replied

Halle took a deep breath "Just grab your stuff and let's get going. We aren't just going to leave you here."

The car ride back was very awkward. Nobody spoke to anyone and Marcos didn't even attempt to start a conversation. Marcos knew deep inside that they wouldn't be in this situation if he didnt say anything. He was still torn about who he wanted to protect and who needed to be thrown under the bus.

As they approached the apartment complex Marcos whispered to them "Let me go inside to clear the area and I'll come back out and give you guys the okay."

Halle looked to Brynn who was sound asleep "I guess all that screaming tired her out." she laughed

Zay turned from the front seat and chuckled
Marcos waved from the top of the staircase
Zed pointed out "Oop that's our signal."

It was weird being back in this house. The apartment layout was very similar to The Carry on Circle just opposite. It almost felt like these homes were a thing of the past even though it had only been three days. That feeling set in of living across the way from here for years making new memories every single day then knowing you can never go back. No closure would come for most of them.

The Carry on Circle avoided stepping into the Mendoza house for months once Antonio started being secretive again. Now this was their only hope.

Nobody could really sleep knowing Gabriel could wake up any minute. Instead they hid away in Marcos' dark room with blankets covering the floor. Thank god the Mendoza's had an unspoken rule about not going into each other's rooms so they didn't have to worry about Gabriel coming in at any time; just getting out would be difficult.

Halle spent the night continuing to stare up at the dark ceiling lit up by the moon light of the open curtains. She knew the only way to keep her sanity was to get out.

Save yourself but what about the people I love. At this point I need to put me first after years of being everyone's mother. The Carry on Circle is going down QUICKLY so it's only a matter of time...

The last of her thoughts until she drifted off to sleep.

9
The Catch

Just as Halle drifted off to sleep, adrenaline woke her up. If she wanted to get out this was her opportunity with no questions asked.

She grabbed what she could from the darkness and snuck out of the room. This could be the last time she saw these people but after years of this exhausting family; it was time to move on.

The sun started to come up. The group collectively woke up around the same time just to realize one of the spaces was empty.

The Carry on Circle exchanged confused looks but ultimately tried to remain quiet. They listened for any sounds of life coming from the rest of the apartment.

Zay whispered "Where did she go?"

"I don't know but that concerns me that you all are still here and she isn't. You guys should have left before the sun came up." Marcos stated

"If she was still in the apartment then we would know." Zay replied

"I think this is our cue to leave then." Zed added

Marcos said "For right now you can leave your stuff here so it doesn't look as suspicious. I can sneak it to you guys if you end up needing it."

The group said their goodbyes and tip-toed out of the Mendoza residence.

"Well now what?" Brynn asked

Zay and Zed shrugged

"I guess we can go to the hang outs for the day and see who's there." Zay said

"Yes, I'm in need of a blunt. This is the longest I've ever been sober!" Zed laughed

The friends crept in the corners of Los Campos. They hopped around from hangout to hang out to pass the time. The longer they ran the more the days became meaningless.

The Carry on Circle that they had put blood, sweat, and tears into for years has officially come to an end. Everyone's main purpose in life was no more. It was almost like Brynn, Zay, and Zed were just floating around in the atmosphere now.

As the hours passed little inconveniences kept getting in the way.

"You know I never noticed that thing before, has that always been there? Do you see it right there?"

Zay looked to Zed with wide annoyed eyes

"Brynn sweetie can't you just be quiet for five minutes please for the love of god I can't take it anymore." Zed stated

"Well that was rude."

"How was that rude?!-" Zed fired back "You've been rambling about random shit all day it's like we have been with a toddler."

"Why is that an issue now? Nobody ever complained before!"

"Because Halle kept us calm." Zay laughed

Zed stopped in his tracks "At this point I don't even know where we are going and i'm tired of walking."

"Yeah me too. I almost feel like we are being watched." Brynn replied

"You're just being paranoid. We need somewhere to rest." Zed said

Zay exclaimed "Okay well I don't know either. Do you two have any ideas?!"

"No, that's why we are asking you?!" Zed responded

"Last time I checked we were a team, it's always been Zay and Zed. Also I don't remember being nominated as the new mom of the group."

Brynn sighed "Halle would know what to do."

"You haven't heard from her at all?" Zed asked

"With what phone- you're right Brynn, Halle would know what to do." Zay stated

"There is a liquor store down the street. I can go get us snacks and maybe a bottle?" Brynn said

The boys exchanged looks and smirked

Zay nodded "Make sure you use a fake just in case."

Zed shouted as Brynn walked off "We will be right here when you get back."

They exchanged looks again

"Run!" they said at the same time

To their surprise the area looked way too familiar. The apartment complex was just down the street!

The two made a beeline for The Carry on Circle apartment. Zay held a single key in his two fingers as they stood in front of the door.

"I'm kinda nervous." Zed said

Zay hovered the key in front of the lock "We can just hide out here for now. If anything we can get some of the things we left behind."

Their jaws dropped as the door swung open. The apartment that used to always be full of people, music, and smoke was now completely empty.

The feelings of lifeless life and dreams taken over by drugs were now only embedded in the walls.

"Wow. completely gutted." Zay whispered

"Wow is right. It's almost sad to see everything gone. We never got closure from this place and it looks like we never will." Zed added

Zay got a pit in his stomach "We should get out of here before anyone sees us. The last thing we want is police on our tail."

The two looked across the way to see an open window to the Mendoza apartment.

"It's our only option." Zay said

Zed shook his head "Marcos warned us."

"I'm willing to take that chance." Zay replied as he made his way up the stairs

Marcos and Gabriel had been talking less and less everyday. The only conversation that filled the house was the sounds from the TV.

Marcos' heart dropped as intense knocking bounced off the door. He began to get up but Gabriel beat him to the door.

"What are you two doing here?! You're lucky i dont call and turn both of you in. you know what you have put my son through! What you have put my family through?!"

Zay stopped the door as Gabriel tried to slam it in their faces "Believe me this is our only option."

"Youcantstayhere." Gabriel said without a stutter "As far as i'm concerned we never saw each other either."

The two made eye contact with Marcos right before the door slammed

"Well what now?" Zed asked

Zay pulled a tiny crumpled piece of paper out of his pocket song with some change "Plan C and my final idea. We need to find a pay phone as quickly as possible."

"Oh there is one at the entrance of the complex!" Zed exclaimed

Zay's heart beated rapidly as he waited for someone to pick up the other line.

Zed listened closely to hear a whole lotta nothing.

The other line whispered into Zay's ear as he mumbled into the pay phone.

Without saying another word he hung up the phone.

Zed waited in anticipation for an answer from Zay "Well?"

Zay answered "He will be here in 20. Brynn should be back by then too."

"I'm sorry, who is *he*?"

Zay grinned, "Someone we know very well."

Zed gasped "Antonio?!"

Zay chuckled "No very close but you will see when he gets here..."

✳✳✳✳

Brynn kicked pebbles down the street to the nearest gas station. All she could think about is losing her best friend. It turns out they really did need her around. *I'm so frustrated with my life. It was never supposed to get to this point. It was just supposed to be fun and finding somewhere I really belonged.*

She reached into her pocket to her surprise was a tiny bag of white powder. She snuck off into a nearby alley where the sun didn't shine. The walk to the gas station was history after that until a rude wake up call came her way...Everything happened faster than the speed of light.

Brynn froze in her tracks. Her life flashed before her eyes as Grace began to put cuffs on her behind her back.

"You never even told me your name?! I'm sorry it has to end like this." Brynn cried

Justin cackled "What?! Sorry princess, you just fell in our trap."

Scott hollered "YEAH! Run now girl!"

"What is going on?!" Brynn asked

Grace guided her to one of the cars "Were you not aware you had a warrant out for your arrest?!"

Brynn didn't have a response

"I don't even think she knows where she is right now." Justin added

Beth got in her face as she sat on the edge of the car "Where are your friends huh?!"

"My friends?"

"Yeah hun where is Halle, and the other two boys. MOST IMPORTANTLY where is Antonio?!"

"I don't know anyone named Antonio."

Beth rolled her eyes "No stop don't even start. Gabriel Mendoza gave YOU up! You were one of the people that he name dropped that we need to get."

Brynn rolled her eyes back "Yeah but that makes me the better person because I didn't rat on anyone."

Scott stated "It makes you dumber! Not better."

"I just do drugs, I'm not a criminal! I don't get how people can do horrific things and get out on probation but I don't even get the option to have mercy."

"Yeah listen when they want someone bigger than you that gives you the opportunity to get yourself out of trouble. Your history from our file is drug addiction and taking part in an identity theft and money laundering ring. You need to be honest about what your part was in The Carry on Circle because if it's just doing drugs they can lessen your sentence." Beth explained "Running was not the answer though."

She snarked, "Whatever, I'm already caught so there's nothing I can do about it now."

"Listen, don't get smart with me or Beth! We are trying to help you in this situation but not if you're being a smart alec."

"I'm going to tell you right now! I am not giving up any information on my friends and I'll do my time."

Beth chuckled, "Spend one night in jail and watch your mindset change."

"I'm sick of this. She's going to jail just like she wants." Scott stated

There was a few minutes of silence then the sounds of sniffles echoed

Brynn began to tear up.

Beth said in a calm voice "Why are you so upset that you're going to jail? Is it because you got caught?"

She sniffled "No I just didn't think I would be doing this by myself. I feel like I lost everyone and I know it's because of my own actions."

"How did you get into the ring?" she asked

"I got kicked out of my house the day after I graduated high school. Which was honestly a miracle that I did complete high school. My parents were almost non-existent during my childhood then started to come back around again once I was old enough to take care of myself. When I was a kid my oldest sister took care of my other older sister and I. She probably was 14 doing the work of two parents. When I finished high school I was the last left in the house and I kid you not the day after my graduation my parents threw me out. I was 18 and found myself in the streets because that's the only place I felt loved. I don't really remember how I met Antonio because I was so high all the time but I know that was a couple years ago and I've been with these people ever since."

"So you just went with the crowd during all the crime?"

"Basically because I was so scared to be disowned by them. Halle joined a little while after me and we became inseparable. She grew out of the drugs but I felt like I kept sinking deeper into them. I always wanted to be like her because she knew better. Now look at me, finally caught up in what I deserve. I'm surprised it took this long."

Scott looked at Beth in the mirror

Somebody had a quick change of heart when reality hit he thought

She took a couple deep breaths and her tears began to dry up when they pulled into the jail parking lot.

****

A beat up car pulled up slowly with the windows still rolled up.

"This has to be our ride." Zay said

"Wait Brynn isn't back yet." Zed replied

Zay looked at his best friend then back at the car "Honestly man it's just you and me now. Brynn will find her way and when we get to a secure location we can get into contact with her. Right now we just have to look out for us because it has always been us!"

Zed nodded then followed Zay to the car. He gasped again as he opened the back door and the driver made eye contact with him.

"Tricky?!"

10

The Last Dime

Gabriel and Marcos jumped out of their skin when an unexpected pounding came from the outside of the front door.

"We got warrants for your arrest. We know you're in there."

Gabriel glared at Marcos "What are they talking about?!"

A panic settled into Marcos' voice "I don't know-?!"

"If you don't open up in 10 seconds we will kick this door in! It's over Marcos."

"Me?!"

"What did you do this time!" Gabriel shouted

"7, 6, 5..."

Marcos leaped over the couch to open the door. His shaky hands reached for the door knob as they hit one.

The boys tackled Marcos and Scott slapped the cuffs on.

"You are under arrest!" Beth yelled

Gabriel tried to intervene but Beth stopped him in his tracks.

"What- What did I do?"

Beth glared at Marcos "I warned you shit was about to get real." she snapped at Justin "Show him."

"Is this not you?" He shouted as he held the fake ID up to his face

"I didn't know about that-" Marcos lied

"Save it. We've heard it all at this point and we have been waitin to put one of you lying bastards in jail!" Scott roared

Gabriel stuttered over his words "This can't be- Marcos I thought you were better-"

"Just shut up Tio, maybe this is a good thing so I can finally escape the mental stress that comes from you!" Marcos exclaimed

All the surrounding neighbors gathered on the pathways to watch the show. The yelling echoed through the walls and soon everyone who lived there was outside. All the residents finally thought it was the day that Antonio was caught but was met with disappointment to see it was Marcos.

Grace and Beth used all their strength to hold Gabriel back.

"Scoot into the middle. My dad and mom will ride with you." Dewy told Marcos

As they approached the cars Beth turned back and yelled "Notice how we are getting closer each time? The next and final time will be your son!"

Gabriel watched as the cars drove away. He thought to himself *I guess I should start making phone calls...well maybe just Antonio deserves to know but the rest will be kept a secret.*

Earlier that morning

Halle's soul was at peace. Walking the empty streets with the birds actually singing instead of hiding. The world was just waking up. This was the time where no problems had come up yet and the misfortunes from yesterday were long gone.

Being away from The Carry on Circle was like a weight being lifted off her shoulders. She loved everyone who belonged with her whole heart but she was at the point that she didn't care what happened to them.

She paced back and forth in front of a pay phone and jingled the change in her hand. She took a deep breath as she put each coin in the phone. Her heart stopped each time the phone dialed then paused then dialed then paused.

"Hello? Who is this?"

"Halle. Is Antonio there?"

"He was just about to head out but i'll let him know you called."

"WAIT-Where is he going? Is he still there?"

"Like I said he was just about to head out and he doesn't have time to talk."

Halle sighed "Just put him on the phone please. He will want to talk if it's me."

There was a long pause with shuffled background noise coming from the other line.

"Hello? Halle?"

"Antonio. We need to talk."

"What's going on? Are you and the crew still coming to the ranch?"

"Well I don't know I left them."

Antonio exclaimed "YOU WHAT?! They won't survive without you."

"Face the music Antonio. The Carry on Circle has fallen apart and I'm tired of running. I thought this lifestyle was for me but I've had a lot of time to think and it's clearly not. I should have left when I got sober years ago but I stayed for you and the family."

"What are you saying." he replied

She replied in a stern voice "This is the last dime I'm spending on you. I'm turning myself in, Antonio."

Antonio paused "Fine. take the selfish route and betray us all."

"If that's how you think about it then you're the problem. Me turning myself in could lead to finally fixing this mess." Halle defended

"I can't believe you're leaving me and the crew all by ourselves. You have been with us for so long and you just wanna give up all the people who care about you? Just to be selfish. I should have known you would have turned on us."

Halle hesitated. She felt the rage build up inside her. All the memories from the past couple years came flooding back. All the times Antonio left them to fend for themselves. All the times they were *supposed to be* a team. All the times Antonio up and left without telling anyone. All the times

Antonio played the victim and blamed the people around him for messing up his life...All the times his family tried to put The Carry on Circle at fault so the problem wouldn't get in trouble.

Why have I been doing this to myself for so long? Why have I given everything to this man who constantly blames me for HIS issues? Enough is enough.

Halle finally responded "I would rather go to jail for the rest of my life then spend enough minute with you and you're fucked up family."

"Halle-"

As soon as she put the phone back she felt another weight lifted off her shoulders.

I had never had this feeling before. Even before The Carry on Circle i felt like i didn't have any freedom because i was trapped by the drug. Although I escaped the drug I ended up getting trapped in the lifestyle. I finally have control of my life!

Antonio held the lifeless phone in his hands

"What just happened?" he said to himself

"What was that about?" one of the guys in the house asked

"The Carry on Circle is falling apart. Anyways, I'm ready to go. My dad and Marcos better have some answers to this."

✳✳✳✳

Gabriel's lifeless arm reached for his phone buzzing on the coffee table

"Dad! Why the hell are authorities calling me non stop and my neighbors are telling me that bounty hunters are showing up at my door almost daily looking for me?!"

"Salia?" Gabriel mumbled

"Oh my god dad are you high? Or maybe I should ask how high are you."

"Dont worry its been taken care of."

"No it certainly hasn't because one you say that every time and two you saying that means something is still going on. What trouble is Antonio in now?"

"He's just on the run again and-"

Salia shouted "HE IS ON THE RUN?! Do you guys not realize my name is tied to his bond? I'm the damn cosigner for christ's sake. I don't have that kind of money to pay for his mistakes."

"They said they have tried calling and you changed your number."

"Well that's odd because I let his bondsman know I was going out of the country and my phone doesn't work when I'm in Mexico. I guess the message didn't translate. What do we have to do to make things right?"

"Well it's already too late because a lot of people are in jail because of Antonio, even Marcos."

There was a sigh on the other line "You let my baby cousin go down because of Antonio. You know dad, I'm done. This has been going on for ten years where I'm always there to save his ass and I can't live my life like this anymore. YOU AND ANTONIO ARE THE PROBLEM! I'm tempted to call the bondsman and ask him to revoke his bond and take me off as a cosigner."

"Salia wait-" Gabriel interrupted

"Dad, no you listen. I have little kids and they have a man in their life who is willing to be their father because their real dad couldn't take it. I do not want my family coming in the way of the family I have created. So here is what we are going to do. I am going to speak to Scott and Beth so we can get this taken care of and I'm going to give them everything they need to settle this. The longer Antonio runs the longer people are going to continue being hurt. Then once this is all settled we are going to pull whatever money we have to find a bondsman for Marcos because HE has actually learned from his mistakes."

Gabriel was silent

"Are you still here?" she asked

Gabriel mumbled some gibberish into the phone

"Good, I'm glad we have an understanding." Salia said

"Dad? Are you okay?"

Gabriel swallowed the pill that was sitting on his tongue "Antonio! What are you doing here? I'm fine son but there is something you should know."

Antonio raised an eyebrow "Where is Marcos?"

Gabriel gulped "I just got off the phone with Salia. She is back home and he seemed very upset. This morning the bounty hunters came and arrested Marcos for identity theft; I guess they found something on him-"

Antonio was quiet, "How did you let this happen."

"Me? We did everything to prevent this." Gabriel argued

"I came here because I needed to know what was going on. Halle called me this morning saying she is turning herself in, then I come here to find my cousin has been arrested now the rest of The Carry on Circle is missing."

"I know it's probably not what you wanted to hear and to make things worse...Salia wants to revoke your bond."

"Why am I the victim in the end of all this?!" Antonio replied "I feel like I'm losing everything."

✳✳✳✳

Halle walked down the main strip of the East Side. Her first steps of freedom but also could be her last. The first time she finally has control of her life is about to be taken again. This time though she had the feeling she was doing something right.

She stood face to face with a glass window and small building that said "Bounty Bail Bonds." The bells on the door jingled as she walked inside.

The lively crowd became silent as she stepped inside. You could hear a pin drop.

Her voice cracked "Hi my name is Halle Burns. I am aware that I am wanted and I am here to turn myself in..."

11

You don't know us

"Get up you lazy bum." a familiar voice said as the door swung open

Antonio lifted his head from slumber "Tricky? You came back? Where the hell have you been?!"

"I was staying with my mom and helping her out. She's not doing to good so I'm debating turning myself in. The only catch is that I don't know how long I'm going in for. I had no idea The Carry on Circle had completely fallen apart too. Did you know?"

"Bro I got cut off from everybody."

Tricky shook his head "And how did that happen? How could *YOU* let that happen?"

"Even my dad hasn't been calling. Marcos is in jail. Maria and my baby are gone. The Carry on Circle is dead. I thought I lost my best friend. I've practically lost everything. I don't even have my freedom anymore because everyone knows I'm wanted."

"End it all and turn yourself in with me. We made a pact that we go down together. I can't keep running."

Antonio didnt have a response

Tricky nodded "Just as I expected. I thought giving you time to think would make you come to your senses but i guess not. Antonio, I've been seeing everything that has been going on around here and all the people who went down for you. There is nobody left besides me! I am not going down for you unless we go down together."

"Maybe we were never as close as I thought."

Tricky chuckled "Get over yourself. This isn't your world anymore!"

Antonio shoved Tricky

He narrowed his eyes "Are you sure you wanna do that? I'm your last bridge that is about to burn. You dug your own grave and it's time you lie in it."

Antonio, again, didn't have a response

"I'm out. It ends here Antonio."

Antonio stood in the empty room by himself as he heard the car drive away on the gravel. The empty room in the empty house with an empty person standing in it. Antonio was officially on his own.

✳✳✳✳

The room was silent as Halle stood in the doorway. It was almost like nobody knew what to do and the shock factor could electrocute you.

Scott's jaw hung open "Uh well hello. Beth, Grace, you know what to do."

Beth handed over her pink cuffs "This one's on you Grace."

"Do you have anything in your pockets that's going to hurt me?" Grace asked

Halle shook her head

"Alright, just keep remaining calm and I'm going to go ahead and search you."

"What made you turn yourself in?" Scott asked

"I was tired of running. I was tired of this life when it served me no good anymore." Halle mumbled

"She's clean." Grace stated

Beth guided her to the couch "We aren't taking you in yet because we need answers."

The biggest smile formed on Scott's face "You realize how long we have been looking for you?! We finally found the ring leader of The Carry on Circle!"

Halle chuckled "I wouldn't say that but I definitely saved their asses from a lot. I don't even know what happened to the ones I called family."

"What made you get into this lifestyle in the first place? Scott asked

"I never was one who got into too much trouble but I found drugs at to young of an age. I grew up in the East side but the part where the sun doesn't shine. I had a good group of friends who were from nice neighborhoods and they could afford to do drugs. We had the mindset that nothing would happen to us and of course being 16 young wild and free drugs were the hottest thing to be getting into. It was only supposed to be fun until it wasn't. I got hooked way faster than my friends did and they didn't like what it brought out of me so soon enough I was on my own. I had an okay family life too and I tried to hide the drugs for as long as I could but eventually they did find out. A lot of those years I can't remember but I know I met Antonio in the streets and he made me feel loved again. I soon grew closer with everyone else and for some reason Antnio trusted me the most so he left me with The Carry on Circle. I had a close call with one of the drugs. I couldn't wait for that high to be over and I knew once I came back down to Earth I would never do hard core drugs again."

"Why did you stay?" Beth asked

"It was the family aspect. I lost everyone because of a mistake I made when I was young. I finally had found people who I vibed with again and I couldn't leave them to fend for themselves."

Dewy joined in "Asking as an inspired person. How were you able to stay in that environment for so long without a relapse?"

"It was hard and at times I was so close but I knew if I did it would end up killing me. Something was keeping me from it though; it was truly a miracle."

Dewy smiled, "God has always been on your side."

Scott replied "He certainly has been. Halle let me ask you this...how old are you?"

"I'm about to turn 25."

He continued "You're at that age where you are still young enough to change your life around before you start getting actual felonies. You are old enough though where you have to decide for yourself what you want to do. If I piss test you right now you're 100% sure it'll come back clean?"

She nodded "I have given you a reason to trust me yet so hopefully this will help a little bit."

"Why does everyone bend over backwards for this guy anyways?" Tim asked

"Lemme put it this way. Antonio wanted an army and what better way to build an army is with control. you rattle up a bunch of people who are dependent on drugs and know you're loyal to them so they can be loyal back. eventually you get so many people on your side it's hard to leave since you're meeting a new family. you'll see less and less of the person who you're worshiping and more of the normal druggies you surround yourself with." Halle explained

"So why did you stay if you're clean?" Dewy asked

"Somehow I worked my way up to a direct line with Antonio with the people he can trust. These people became my family over the years and I can't let them go. we all found each other at our lowest and brought out the best in each other..."

Scott and Tim rummaged through the cabinet

Halle and Dewy kept glancing over at each other. There was something about him. His smile?

His eyes? His demeanor? She couldn't help but get butterflies.

She thought to herself: But *why, this was the enemy...right?! Who am I kidding? I'm the one sitting here in handcuffs right now. He must think all sorts of awful things about me.*

Justin asked "Why would you want to become a god awful person though?"

"Hey man, chill out." Dewy chimed in

"Bro she's a fugitive sitting in handcuffs right now." Justin argued

"Yeah but she isn't putting up a fight. Not all of them can be bad. If anything most fugitives just need help."

Halle spoke up "He's right. You don't know us. We aren't all bad."

Scott threw the test on the couch "Here. Grace will supervise."

Grace closed the door behind them "I know this is probably super awkward and weird but you're safe here."

Halle smiled and proceeded to unbox the test. She could hear chatting coming from the main room that she just knew was about her.

Her heart raced as they waited for the test results to come in. With every possible scenario playing in her head: *What if something was slipped into my drink or food? What if being around drugs caused me to still have substances in my system? What if it traveled through the air? What if being*

around it for so long never really made me as
sober as I thought? What if...

"It's negative!" Grace shouted from the bathroom

Halle sighed a relief. Finally a foundation of trust is being built.

Scott ordered Dewy to take her to the cars in the back. As Dewy reached for Halle's arm a shock came through. They both slightly gasped as they made eye contact.

He brushed it off as he opened the back door "Do you smoke?"

Halle nodded "Just cigs nowadays."

Dewy pulled out a small cardboard box from his pocket "We have to keep you cuffed until we get to the jail but it should be manageable in the front."

Halle put the dry cigarette in her mouth as Dewy reached for his lighter. The two of them made intense eye contact as Dewy shared a flame with Halle. She looked up into his eyes that seemed to be glistening. For some reason the same energy he radiated was relatable. Almost like he was hiding pain behind that bullet proof vest.

They took turns blowing smoke away from each other's faces. They didn't say much, just lived in the moment.

Soon enough the rest of the crew joined them outside. The women: Beth, Felicia, and Grace went in one car with Halle then the men in the second.

"We thought it would be less intimidating to have just women." Felicia said as she got in the car

Beth turned to Halle "There is something different about you compared to any other fugitive we have caught. Not even talking about this case either. I don't feel right about throwing you in jail and forgetting about you. You are smart, beautiful, and have too much potential to throw it away. Everyone makes mistakes and it seems like you learned from them a long time ago. That's why we discussed it and we want to put you on bond with us."

"Thank you so much!" Halle cheered

"Now that doesnt mean go run and tell everyone because this is a rare occurrence. Nobody ever jumps bail on us so if you're planning on pulling something you might as well just stay in the cell. This was my idea and it's been tough convincing my hunny so you better not make me look stupid." Beth stated

Felcia chimed in "You know I never had daughters so when Scott met Beth and brought her into the family we grew very close. Then when I gained Grace as a granddaughter it was even better. When we met Beth she was just getting sober and getting her life on track. She reminded me a lot of myself when I met Tim and right now you are reminding me a lot of her. For some odd reason you tie perfectly into this family."

"Thank you for taking a chance on me. I promise I will do everything to make this right and I want to do what I need to do to take care of this." Halle responded

I never thought I would be seeing the Los Campos Jail with my own eyes let alone be setting foot in it. I just know people already hate me in there. Also who knows what story Brynn has been giving. I've wronged a lot of people under Antonio's influence now it's time to make things right.

Scott called for Grace to walk her inside but Dewy closely followed behind

"Dad didn't ask you to come." Grace said

Dewy glanced to Halle "Well maybe I'm tired of following dads orders."

Grace shrugged and whispered to Halle "And they make *me* out to be the dramatic one."

She rang the doorbell "Grace Bounty, here dropping off fugitive Halle Burns."

A violent buzz with a spiritless tone. A cold draft from inside greeted them as they entered.

As the doors locked behind Halle and the Bounty kids departed that feeling set in of where she was. Most people might think it's not that serious until you get caught but even when she was roaming free it was never fun and games.

Right before she passed through the gates she glanced over her shoulder to see Dewy still standing at the door. Even through these stone cold walls a ray of sunshine was shining in.

The rest of that day was fuzzy. The booking and processing process took almost 4 hours to complete before Halle was thrown into the fire.

The next few days were in and out of cells and the facility to finish up paperwork. Since Beth had promised to provide bail for Halle that gave her a sliver of hope she would make it out of here.

The Los Campos Jail was your typical gloomy facility with two levels of cells for each floor then the day room being in the middle with circular metal picnic tables. It was rare if you knew someone that you would be on the same floor, especially if it was common knowledge to the court that you guys had ties.

Completely by chance Brynn was on floor 6...and so was Halle.

Kaydon was still somewhere in the jail too. The facility sat right next to the larger than life court house and had two identical buildings. One for men and one for women.

As soon as Halle entered the day room for the first time all eyes were on her. She had a huge target on her back for various reasons. The obvious being tied to the Carry on Circle. Also her being new to the system and of course just because she's fortunate looking. The feeling of anger by others followed her as she walked through the room. On the other hand she had a reputation of being one of the only good higher ups in the Carry on Circle who was there not the people and not the business. A familiar face sitting at one of the tables shined through everyone.

Halle's heart raced as she approached the table. She had heard many stories so she wasn't completely new to the unspoken rules. She was just worried how this would come across to the veterans "Can we talk?" she asked the girl

"What are you doing here?"

"Brynn I am so sorry for everything that has happened."

She shook her head "No Halle I made it so much more difficult than it needed to be. Being in here gives you a lot of time to think. Plus Scott and Beth put a lot of things into perspective."

Halle smiled "Who would have thought we would be sitting here together after we were both promised we would never get caught."

Brynn chuckled "The years we spent in The Carry on Circle feels like a lifetime ago."

...Line up ladies

"I'm on the other side so i don't know how much we will see each other but free time i'm usually here!"

Halle responded "Perfect I'll see you back here!"

Halle thought to herself *It's like she's a completely different person. This is the Brynn I remember becoming best friends with.*

12

Like a villain

Salia threw the car in park as she ran up to her family's place.

Gabriel dropped his spoon into his soup once the door swung open.

"Ay hija me asustaste." Gabriel gasped

"Sorry dad, I didn't mean to frighten you."

"What are you doing coming in like that?"

Salia raised an eyebrow "Because I used to live here? Come on, we are going grocery shopping. We need to get you outta the house."

"But what if the bounty hunters come back?" Gabriel asked

"Marcos' buddies are down in the parking lot. We will let them know to phone us if anything happens."

"What if Antonio comes by when we are here?"

Salia reassured "He won't and if he did I would have something to say about it."

A couple hours went by with nothing happening. It's almost like Gabriel jinxed himself though because right as the clock struck 12 the phone rang. His shaky hands held the phone and Salia motioned to answer. Right as he pushed answer, the call ended.

"That's not good." he said

"It's okay, don't freak out, I'm sure it's nothing. They'll find nothing." Salia said in a stern voice

Gabreil reached in his pocket and pulled out a white pill

"Absolutely not, you're not doing that here. How does that make me look like a good daughter when my dad is getting high in the store."

Gabriel threw it on his tongue without a second thought "How is the familia?"

"Well my kids are great, the husband is great, we were all great in Mexico when we didn't have to deal with this Antonio bull shit. They ask me "mama why are you so stressed out all of a sudden?" Little do they realize it's their beloved uncle who they think is so innocent."

'Lower your voice sweetie."

She laughed "Lower my voice?! It's not like everyone around here hasn't been giving us dirty looks already. The familia down in the village wishes Antonio was behind bars already."

Gabriel put his hand to his forehead "I'm tired i think i'm ready to go home."

Salia loaded the groceries onto the belt and muttered something to herself.

As they got back to the complex Marcos' buddies were still outside working on the car. They motioned for them to come over.

"Aye those ops were here again. I tried calling but they snatched my phone before I could answer. They knew we called you but saw you weren't home. They said something about going over to Salia's." one of the men said

"Great, now I have to deal with this. I'm not going home yet. They can hang out all they want but nobody is there to answer to them." Salia scoffed

A couple hours had passed. Salia thought she would try her luck with the Bounty's being gone. Her car was pretty recognizable with being associated with her brother's clan. Pitch black tint and blinding rims made her stand out like a sore thumb. As soon as she turned the corner she saw two big black SUVs surrounding her house with people in the street.

"Shit we need to get out of here." Salia whispered to her husband

"But why? I thought you were tired of this?"

Salia whipped a U-turn in one of the driveways "Yeah but that doesn't mean i'm ready to deal with it on my own. I can be all talk but when it comes down to it I'm not ready to let go of my brother. It's getting too real."

Her husband gripped onto the seat "Slow down Salia it's going to be okay."

"We have to get far enough where we can lose them." She looked into her rearview mirror to see one of those black cars following close behind her. "Damn it!" she cried and turned into a dead end road "I can't avoid this any longer."

Salia's heart raced as a masculine figure and a flashlight approached closer to her car.

She slightly opened the door with her hands up with the white flag.

The man reached for his radio "Chased down the car and now I'm sitting with Antonio's sister at the dead end by Summerville Rd." he opened the door all the way "Step out of the car Salia this has gone on too long!"

She watched as Dewy shined his flashlight into her husband's face.

"My dad will be on the way shortly." Dewy said

"Salia! Where is your brother?!" Scott yelled as he hopped out of the car

"Scott I don't know. I have been in Mexico for the past month."

Beth chimed in "Then why did your phone number say it was out of service when we tried to reach you."

"My phone doesnt work outside of the States. I let Antonio's bondsman know that but I guess he didn't relay the message."

Scott responded "He most certainly did not but listen we found check and prescription paper in your trash which is public domain. Plus your neighbors said Antonio had been around during the time you were gone."

"I made it clear he was not welcome in my home or in the neighborhood!" Salia defended

"Well look how far that got you." Beth snarked

"Listen I am trying to work this out and I only found out what's going on when the authorities were calling me non stop." Salia said

"Have you spoken to your dad?" Scott asked

"And you never answered my question on why you were driving so crazy if you were innocent!" Dewy chimed in

"I talked to my dad yesterday and he told me about Marcos getting arrested and I said we need to put an end to this. I have always taken the blame for so many of my family members and I have had a clean record. I am tired of saving my younger brother's ass all the time. My dad knows more about this than I do. I have kids I need to take care of. I don't want to be a part of this. "

Salia's husband glanced at her with her pants being on fire. She stood strong and looked them dead in the face.

Beth shrugged "Okay, lets just take her over to Gabriel's then and let them talk it out."

Her husband sighed as she got back in "Why would you lie? You literally just came from your dads place. You're digging your grave deeper."

"I know I know but it's hard not to lie. I've been doing it for so long and been covering it up with the good girl act."

"Just be careful. I don't want to lose you because you're protecting your brother."

Salia was leading the pack. Pulling up to the condo complex and unlike before the Mendoza house was completely dark.

As soon as Gabriel opened the door Salia shook her head "Papá, no podemos seguir viviendo así. Antonio has put us through hell and back so it's time to let him go."

There was a silence after the bounty hunters left. Salia was the first to speak

"Dad." Salia sighed, "Tricky was a part of the family."

"What's done is done."

"You know where Antonio is then. Because if he was still at the ranch you wouldn't have given them the address."

"You aren't even better!" Gabriel yelled "You were lying to their faces and continued to protect him. Besides, Tricky isn't and will never be blood."

Salia looked him dead in the eyes "The next time they come in here i'm telling them im done. I choked when I was actually thrown into the fire. It's an instinct to protect family no matter what...even if it's the same person all the time! I'm sticking to my original word."

13
Tricky

I grew up in the Westside of Los Campos.
Being a part of that growing up made me the person
I am today. There are a lot of secrets to this city,
more than people want to realize. The South and
North side have big business mafia's and money
laundering filtering in and out. The East side has
it's troubles too but it was the place where more
families resigned. The west side is somewhere that
nobody wanted to be. The population continues
here by being born into it.

My dad was a part of 19th West which is the
biggest gang in Los Campos. Naturally I grew up in
the streets because that's what I was accustomed to.
My dad was someone I never wanted to be like. I
always hated the color green because of what he
was a part of. At nine years old I was practically the
man of my house who needed to protect my mom
and younger sister. What my dad was doing?...I
would rather not say but it made me see a lot of
shit.

I met Antonio in the streets of the East side.
It's funny because everyone likes to say the North

and South sides are best friends while the West and East just need to learn to tolerate each other. Me Personally I don't know where they got that saying but I found my east side boy.

My deadbeat dad ended up dead on my 14th birthday. Happy Birthday to me right...welcome to manhood.

One of the things that Antonio and I bonded over was losing a parent. It's something we had to choke down especially because we are both men. The difference between us is I grew up raised by women while Antonio grew up raised by his older brother and dad. His poor sister, Salia never could have caught a break even if it killed her.

I loved my family but slowly I drifted away from them when Antonio and I got closer. I practically became a Mendoza myself.

Then The Carry on Circle formed and it wasn't just us two anymore.

I never was too fond of everything that was going on but we made a killing off it. This was always Antonio's thing but everyone quickly attached me to it.

At this point you may be wondering what happened to Zay and Zed...

"Tricky?!" Zed gasped as he opened the car door

"Quick get in, I don't want anyone to see you guys. While we are here I need to talk to Gabriel." Tricky said

"We just came from there and he made it very clear we were not welcomed." Zay said

"That's fine you guys can wait in the car. I won't be long." Tricky made his way up the stairs with his hood on. With the Mendoza's and Carry on Circle being located here you know someone is constantly looking out their window all the time.

Tricky opened the door without knocking

Startled, Marcos asked "Tricky? What are you doing here?"

"I'm going to make this quick, i'm planning on turning myself in tomorrow morning. Tonight I'm staying at the ranch and packing the last bit of my belongings up to take to my moms." Tricky said

"Woah woah turn yourself in? How could you be so selfish?" Gabriel asked

"Yeah Tricky maybe you're jumping the gun. We can get ourselves out of this." Marcos added

He shook his head "It's me they want not all of you...it's *Antonio and I* they want and not all the people you let go down for us."

"How did you find out?" Gabriel asked

"You must think I'm stupid. Unlike you guys, the people of The Carry on Circle actually trust me. They used to feel the same way about Marcos but look where you're standing now."

"Hey man this is family-" Marcos chimed in

Tricky cackled "Family. You guys wouldn't even know what that word means. We considered each other family but just because I'm not blood you tossed me out. Face the music! Antonio is going down one way or another."

"I thought you were his running mate and would do anything for him." Gabriel snarked

Tricky answered "No you have that completely twisted. Antonio and I would do anything for eachother and if one of us went down then we went down together. Clearly that pact doesn't apply here where he would give me up in a heartbeat."

Marcos and Gabriel didn't my respond

Tricky shrugged, "Well I see I've overstayed my welcome."

"How did that go?" Zed asked as Tricky opened the car door

He shook his head "I hate that I've wasted so much time on these people."

As they drove out of the complex Zay exclaimed "Oh my god! Look!"

"Those are the same cars that we saw that night at the motel!" Zed added

Tricky looked at the two big blacked out cars driving in the complex "What WHAT?! Do you guys mean?!"

"We need to get out of here now!" Zay yelled

Tricky's foot met the gas pedal and they sped off. "Where would you guys want me to drop you off?" he asked

Zay and Zed exchanged looks

"The trapper house?" Zed suggested

"Okay that's fine but after this I have to cut ties. You guys have always been real ones and ima miss you homies but it's safer for us to go our separate ways." Tricky replied

The two nodded

Zay said "We appreciate everything you have done for us!"

Tricky pulled in front of the house that was just down the street "And I could say the same thing to do. Thank you for keeping the Carry on Circle together."

Things were getting serious. I was officially on my own but I didn't mind that. I never had an encounter with Scott and Beth until just now. Thinking back to the past couple of weeks where they never reached out to me, they never tried calling me, they never asked any of my informats. I don't even think they called my cosigner.

Could this be a good thing or a bad thing? Maybe I'm not as wanted as I thought I was and I'm going to turn myself in for no reason. But also they can be hunting in silence...they aren't doing that with Antonio though? I could easily get out of this- no i'm making excuses. I've grown so much as a person where I don't want this lifestyle anymore.

Before I knew it I was back at the ranch. I had made this drive so many times in the couple months I've been staying here. Everything always looked like a picture. Nothing ever changing or moving.

Who actually owned this property was unknown to us. Whoever owns it though sure knows what they are doing. All the cars that can be visible when you get closer is just a deception. They tried to make it as scary as possible so people wouldn't bother us. Why would they...a huge run down ranch with multiple cars on the very edge of town. Yeah that seems safe.

I didn't have many things still at the house but I needed to move my possibly potentially illegal things. Plus I had some personal belongings that I knew were safe here that I needed to pass to my mom.

This was a rare occurrence where nobody except me was home.

I faintly heard the sound effect of motion detected right at the entrance of our road. Usually these are just rabbits crossing but this time felt different. There could have been multiple what ifs. I think I made a mistake by telling the Mendoza's my plan.

I snuck into the bedroom of one of the main gangsters here...I know, bad idea...but that's where the hidden cameras are at. The quality wasn't good but it told me enough. I felt my heart sink as two big black cars kicked up dust pulling closer to the house. I knew I had about two minutes to think of a plan.

There are the locked sheds in the back, or the closets, maybe under the bed. What a curse to make the house seem like someone was always home. I guess the leaders didn't anticipate ever getting raided.

I heard the tires on the gravel getting closer to the house. I couldn't help but panic.

It is one of those moments where you are serious about your act until it happens when you aren't ready then your walk becomes all talk.

I heard footsteps surrounding the house but I was frozen in the bedroom. Thankfully all the curtains were closed and the doors were locked.

There was only one way in and that was through kicking the door or breaking a window.

All of a sudden an earth shaking pounding came from the door.

..."We have warrants for your arrest boy! We have the house surrounded and sheds surrounded so don't even try to run."

A woman's voice yelled "You have 30 seconds before we kick this door in."

Then another one from the window outside of the bedroom I was in

"Someone is shuffling in the back bedroom!"

"Shit shit shit." I whisper to myself as I scramble around in the bedroom

Without a second thought I slid underneath the bed and barricaded myself with clothes and other objects. As soon as I exhaled there was the sound of a crash in the front of the house.

"Search this place good!" a man hollered

I counted my blessings one by one. What was I even doing? I should have just come out peacefully when I still had time.

I made that impulsive decision because once a criminal always a criminal. It's your instrict to always find a way to protect yourself and avoid the consequences.

I heard footsteps get closer to the doorway and enter the room I was in. I held my breath as one of the guys walked around the bed. Then it got silent. I heard the sound of pants rub together as he crouched.

The flashlight from a gun swifted from each side of the bed then to the middle. The light shined through the clothes and into my eyes. When the light stayed in the same spot for a minute I knew it was over.

"HE IS RIGHT HERE!" he yelled

All of a sudden it went from one to four people dragging me out from underneath the bed.

All four of them were cheering but I felt numb inside. I laid face down on the disgusting carpet. I felt the point of a gun in my back.

Two of them lifted me up and I was able to see Scott Bounty standing right in front of me. To my left was one of his sons Dewy, then on my right was his other son, Justin. It was haunting how much they all looked like Jacob.

They cuffed me in the front and guided me outside. I internally said goodbye to what was my home.

Justin stopped in the doorway and asked where Antonio was.

That I wish I could answer.

Beth shook my hand and wasn't cruel at all. She began showing me everyone Gabriel gave up in place for his son and now my name would be added to that list. The Bounty's were so calm with me and not at all how I expected.

A part of me wanted to give them everything I knew but I still had love for Antonio. He was my brother through everything. I just don't think I could give him up even if I had the information to.

With going to jail and making things right that means I am getting another chance at life. That should be something Antonio decides for himself if he wants that or not.

I guess his situation is different.

When I got to the jail it wasn't new at all. I had been in and out a couple times before. This time I didn't know how long I was staying.

Everyone seemed to know me and already respect me. In a way I feel like I didn't deserve it.

I made a beeline for Marcos in the dayroom. Maybe this wasn't a good idea because I let my emotions get the best of me.

I saw the fear in his face as I got closer.

I whispered to him "If we weren't wearing jumpsuits and being watched by guards I would beat the living piss out of you. You are a damn coward Marcos Mendoza. You spent all that time throwing other people under the bus and look where it got you. You dug your own grace and now you're lying in it."

He looked me dead in the eyes but didn't respond.

I muttered "Stay far away from me I don't wanna see you even in the distance for as long as we are in here. I used to ride for your family and now you're dead to me. Once people start figuring out you're a mendoza it's over for you."

I felt a weight be lifted off my shoulders as I backed away. My story was complete for now. Jail was my second chance and from this day forward I'm pushing the reset button.

I made a lot of mistakes in my ast and I'm sure the future won't be easy. I'm not dead yet and that's all that matters.

14
So we meet again

The phone ringing broke the silence in the room. Gabriel was in and out of sleep but Salia was wide awake. Her anxiety kept her conscious.

Her husband motioned for her to answer

Before she could even say hello, Beth rapidly said "Are you still at your dads?"

"Yes."

"Good stay right there we are on our way."

Then the call ended

Salia rubbed her eyes "It's almost 11 what could they possibly need now!"

"Just give them what they want, Salia." Her husband muttered

She asked "And what would that be?"

"You already know! And you know how to reach him by cell."

"Okay okay i'll call him and see if he answers."

✳✳✳✳

Antonio sat by himself on a vacant park bench. The fog could be seen through the dim street lamps. The world was still and at peace.

He was officially on his own. He couldn't turn back to Tricky after he had abandoned him. He couldn't help but think they were supposed to be brothers. He couldn't turn back to his family because they abandoned him too.

The people who I loved the most are no longer with me. The last time I talked to my dad he informed me that he let my cousin go to jail. The last time I talked to my sister she wanted no part of me. Who cares right I don't need them. I don't need anyone! I've been fighting this battle by myself and I've never had anyone be loyal to me. My heart aches for all the betrayal I've suffered.

Just then something in his pocket buzzed

He pulled out his tiny phone to see Salia's number calling. He laughed and powered off the phone.

"They wanna reach out now after they have wronged me. There is no way that's happening." he scoffed

✳✳✳✳

Suddenly headlights shined in through the curtains .

"It's your decision what you wanna do."

"I don't know why he isn't answering." Salia cried "There is nothing more I can do."

Then the door opened

"So we meet again." Scott said

Gabriel jumped up from his sleepy trans "WHO IS HERE?!"

"Relax Gabriel, it's just us." Beth said in an annoyed tone

"Any word from Antonio?" Tim asked

Salia shook her head "I tried calling him and he didn't answer."

Beth paused "Wait what? You have contact with him?!"

Salia looked to her husband for support

"This is on you!" he said

Salia nodded slightly "He has a trap phone that my dad has been in contact with. Other than that he's always just reached out to me." Tears began to roll down her face "Scott Beth i'm being so truthful right now. I'm sorry I lied to protect him before. Please believe me now! If he doesn't come in tonight you can arrest me."

Beth sat down next to Salia. In a calm voice she said "Okay we aren't going to do that but now we know that you're agreeing to help us."

She agreed "Yes it's the least I can do now. I know I'm not innocent because he is my brother but I want to help."

"Here is the plan. You are going to call him and in the most panicked voice say you can't go back to the ranch because dad ratted it out to the bounty hunters so you aren't safe there." Beth explained

"But- he isn't answering."

Gabriel butted in "Yeah he won't answer-"

Beth continued "Then you repeatedly call him until he does answer. And leave voice mails so he believes this is real."

Salia breathed deeply "Okay. then what?"

"I don't think this is going to work." Gabriel interrupted

"Dad, please. let them finish." Salia said

Scott chimed in "You're going to tell him that Scott and Beth just arrested Tricky and took him to jail so you can hide out here. If anyone finds out your dad ratted out their hiding spot you're a dead man!"

"I don't know if i can do this."

"It will be more believable coming from you than your dad. You can have that concern in your voice!" Felicia said

"Our final step is staging. We will have to scope out every possible area to make sure Antonio doesnt see us but we can see his every move." Scott said "Plus we will have to stage you and your dad to make you guys look natural."

"Either way once he's in the building he can't run anywhere." Justin said

"Alright, the boys and I will go scope out the whole complex and look for hiding spots while the girls sit here with Salia and feed her the script." Scott ordered

❋❋❋❋

The minutes passed which felt like hours. Antonio had no way to get back to the ranch but at the same time he didn't want to. He was appreciating the solitude. It's almost like he felt his story coming to an end. He knew deep down this was the start of a new beginning where he would now have to fight all his battles on his own.

For the first time since he was a child he was sober. His common misconception was he needed to be high in order to function. Maybe it was the cold air or the lack of smoke…the world actually seemed clear for once.

"Antonio?" a woman's voice said

Antonio formed a smile "Mama? What are you doing here? How are you here?"

"I heard you were in trouble. My son, I love you but you need to do what's right."

"Mama, I haven't done anything. Don't you see everyone turned their back on me."

She sat down next to him "I always worried you would turn out like your brother. You turned out like the person I never wanted you to be. Selfish, cruel, a bastard, and the worst of a villain."

Antonio, for the first time since he lost his mom actually felt something internally. He had forgotten what pain was, what joy was, what any basic human emotion was.

Antonio jerked awake. His clothes and the bench were covered in sweat. His mouth was incredibly dry and his heart felt like it was going to pop out of his chest.

As soon as he got up he fell to the floor. It felt like a knife stabbed him in his stomach.

I've done enough to this world so if it was to take me out that would be okay.

It took all his strength to drag himself up against the bench

As soon as he powered it on, tens of messages and missed calls came from Salia.

..."Mano you can't go back to the ranch tonight! It isn't safe for you to return. Tricky was arrested by the bounty hunters and by now I'm sure everyone knows dad was the one who ratted the ranch out."

One by one he listened to each message

What was even real at this point? I can see right through my hands and I feel like my intestines are going to fall out. I have no choice but to go running back to my dad and sister who has always bailed me out. He thought to himself

He didn't have the strength to hold himself up anymore. He laid on his back under the stars with his mind drifting off to sleep.

The phone remained in his hand and after a few minutes it buzzed again.

Salia was calling again.

Antonio could only lift his thumb but this time there actually was an answer.

"Antonio?!" Salia said

He breathed heavily into the phone "Salia I think i'm dying-"

"WHAT?!" she shouted "Where are you?!"

He didn't respond

"Antonio, I'm not messing around, I will come get you. Just tell me where you are!"

The brightness of the phone blinded him as he checked to see the battery life.

1%.

He muttered into the phone "I love you and tell dad I love him too."

"No Antonio I am not letting you do this! Think of all the people who still love you. Mom would want to see you live!" Salia exclaimed

Antonio's eyes widened. He lifted his head to see an outline of a familiar building behind him. He stuttered "Oh- my god. SALIA- I amm already herre."

"What?" She asked

Then the line disconnected

"Damn it !" Antonio shouted as he looked at the dead phone

My mom died but why should I have to. He thought *I have made a lot of wrongs but it's time to fix those.*

He used all the strength he regained to pull himself to his feet.

He stares intensely at the entrance of the Condo complex. He had a feeling of it officially being the end. It's almost like he would step foot in his dads house and die with the people he loves.

He finally made it to the bottom of the staircase. He took a deep breath as he put one foot above the other.

About half way up he had to use his hands to crawl up the rest of the way.

He was nose to nose with the door, back on his feet.

Salia got up from the couch to welcome him in but faster of the speed of light his life stopped.

"FREEZE!"

15
The Final

One minute Antonio had the strength to stand then the next moment 3 men tackled him to the floor.

It was officially 1am and way past the complex's quiet hours.

Everyone was screaming at the top of their lungs cheering but also at Antonio.

He laid face down on the floor. Defeated.

Salia rushed over to check on him while Gabriel remained in the corner

"He is burning up! Babe get me a cold towel!" Salia shoutted

"Okay this isn't good because we can't take him to jail like this." Scott said

"Why not? We caught him, isn't that what matters?" Justin said

"No, we can't just let him suffer in there." Dewy added

"That's the other part of being a bounty hunter...having a heart. That's where you and your brother differ in skill." Scott explained "Roll him over so she can care for him." he ordered

Salia crouched down and placed the cool towel on his forehead.

Once in a while Antonio would cold shiver but didn't have anything to say.

Salia turned to Antonio "I'm sorry brother I had to do this for your safety and our family."

Antonio lifted his head and looked into her eyes. He slowly looked at everyone one by one, lastly at his dad then back at his sister.

He shouted "HOW COULD YOU LET THIS HAPPEN?!"

Salia felt pricks in the back of her eyes

Antonio tried to get up but his body weighed him down. He continued yelling "THIS NEVER WOULD HAVE HAPPENED-"

"Okay NOPE." Scott shouted as him and the boys picked him up off the ground

"YOU AREN'T GOING TO TALK TO A WOMAN LIKE THAT!" Scott yelled back

Antonio began laughing "You wouldn't know the first thing about that."

He shook his head "Really? You wanna go there? Justin, Dewy take him down to the cars."

Salia's tears rolled down her face as she watched her brother be taken away in handcuffs.

Gabriel hasn't said one word throughout this whole thing.

One by one they headed out the condo and down the stairs. Scott and Tim were the last two with Gabriel.

"You sure suck as a father." Tim said

Scott scoffed as well "To see your son suffer like that and you do nothing...he should be the one who gets to walk free because his father is a monster!"

The door slammed behind the Bounty's and now Gabriel once again was alone in the condo.

There was no saying what he might do or what might happen to him but it's probably not going to be a fairy tale ending.

Salia's husband hugged her tight as they loaded Antonio into the car.

When given the clear she walked to the edge of the car and whispered "i'm afraid you wont make it. Our family has made a lot of enemies who are paying the price for us. If you don't believe in God you better start now and beg him to have mercy."

Antonio kept looking forward but replied "If I was afraid I wouldn't have done half the things i've done." he lowered his voice "I am a believer now because he let me say goodbye to mom."

"What?" Salia asked

"We need to roll out. Family say your final goodbyes then we will be on our way." Scott told

Salia hugged him one last time and her husband did a nod of acknowledgement.

She whispered something in his ear so quiet only a mouse could hear.

"Don't worry your legacy will be kept alive. Everything always works out for us so this is just a little ripple in the water. Dad will find a way to get you out."

Antonio didn't smile just nodded once

Scott and Beth sat in between Antonio

He couldn't help but worry a little bit.

Beth tried to start small talk but was successful.

Scott chuckled "You truly are a dog man. They say drug addicts are not smart but you are the hardest we ever have had to hunt for someone."

Antonio grinned, "It's an art. You wouldn't know anything about it though."

"Okay smart ass. You know what I shouldn't be showing mercy on you considering what happened but that would get us nowhere."

Antonio knew exactly what he meant. It wasn't the long chase or running a muck around the city. It was Jacob.

Antonio responded "I didn't think I would ever have the chance or heart to say this but I'm sorry about what happened to Jacob. He was one of my best friends and what happened was never supposed to happen."

"Never did I think I would hear those words either. Antonio I know I can't forgive you but at the same time it's been over a decade and the only way to move on and heal is to forgive. I'll admit I wanted you dead from the beginning but I can only wish you the best."

As they pulled up to the jail, Antonio felt a lump in his throat. He had promised so many people that they would never be here even though he knew deep down he could guarantee that promise. He would throw anyone under the bus to go to the slammer in order to keep himself out of there. Never did he think he would be back here doing real time.

Scott and Beth helped him out of the car. As both of his feet plotted on the jail's property he had this unsettling feeling. It's like he could already hear the bangs and screams coming from inside the cells of people waiting for his arrival. His footsteps were pounding in his ears with every step he took.

The pain of withdrawal still present and fate about to come he felt himself wanting to pull away.

What would happen if he broke free from Scott and Justin holding him and just took off running? What if he ran so fast they couldn't catch him? What if he could get a second chance on his life?

All of that sounded nice but as the door opened and the jail air hit him; he had to forget all his past tactics.

The guard's jaws were to the floor when Antonio took his first steps into intake.

Never did they think they would see the day where Antonio would be entering a jail.

No matter how hard it was going to be, Antonio promised himself that he wanted to be a changed man. Getting clean and doing time would be the way to fix that. Once he completes his sentence he won't even be recognizable as Antonio Mendoza...At least that's what he was going to tell the judge ;)

The End

The Characters:

I get asked all the time why I put pictures in my stories. This time I tried to stay away from that but I found out recently it can actually be appreciated by people who can't visualize while reading. I started doing it because I thought it was a cool and different concept but now I know it actually can be helpful. With that being said here is a glimpse into my mind on how I visualized the characters looking but still giving you that freedom to determine that on your own :)

Check out honeybbrooke's other work:

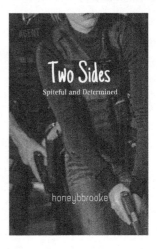

A Message From The Author:

You did it! You have reached the end! Depending on if you read the stories at the same time or if you started with this one I would love to hear your feedback. When writing this I thought this would be a super difficult concept to actually make work but the story just fell into place. Like I say with every story...the characters and the story write itself. I am incredibly proud of how 4&5 turned out and I couldn't have envisioned them better. Sometimes I feel a little bit of doubt at the end if that's how I envisioned the story going but I didn't feel that with this story. I can't wait to see what opportunities this story could bring in the future. Thank you for following along on this journey and reading my latest adventures.

Made in the USA
Las Vegas, NV
15 April 2024